Ordinary Decent Criminal

ALGARVE
BOOK   € 5
CELLAR

PRICE
REFUND
2

GRETTA CURRAN BROWNE was born and grew up in Dublin city. She left Dublin as a teenager, and went to London to study drama. She started writing in January 1984 and had two articles and a short story published, which encouraged her to start writing her first novel, *Tread Softly on My Dreams*. It was reissued by Wolfhound Press in 1998, as was her second novel, *Fire on the Hill*. Her contemporary novel, *Ghosts in Sunlight*, was published by Wolfhound Press in 1999.

KEVIN SPACEY   LINDA FIORENTINO
ORDINARY DECENT CRIMINAL
ICON ENTERTAINMENT INTERNATIONAL PRESENTS
A LITTLE BIRD PRODUCTION IN ASSOCIATION WITH
TATFILM AND TRIGGER STREET PRODUCTIONS
A FILM BY THADDEUS O'SULLIVAN
KEVIN SPACEY LINDA FIORENTINO PETER MULLAN and STEPHEN DILLANE
ORDINARY DECENT CRIMINAL
HELEN BAXENDALE DAVID HAYMAN PATRICK MALAHIDE GERARD McSORLEY
Casting Directors ROZ AND JOHN HUBBARD
Original Score Composed by DAMON ALBARN
Costume Designer JANE ROBINSON Production Designer TONY BURROUGH
Editor WILLIAM ANDERSON ACE Director of Photography ANDREW DUNN BSC
Co-Producer MARTHA O'NEILL
Executive Producers JAMES MITCHELL and CHRISTINE RUPPERT
Screenplay by GERARD STEMBRIDGE
Producer JONATHAN CAVENDISH Directed by THADDEUS O'SULLIVAN
Produced in association with MIRAMAX FILMS, BORD SCANNÁN NA hÉIREANN/
THE IRISH FILM BOARD, THE GREENLIGHT FUND, FILMSTIFTUNG NRW

Ordinary Decent Criminal

a novel by

Gretta Curran Browne

Based on the film starring
KEVIN SPACEY and LINDA FIORENTINO

WOLFHOUND PRESS
Celebrating 25 *Years*

First published in 2000 by
Wolfhound Press Ltd
68 Mountjoy Square
Dublin 1, Ireland
Tel: (353-1) 874 0354
Fax: (353-1) 872 0207

Wolfhound Press receives financial assistance from The Arts
Council/An Chomhairle Ealaíon, Dublin, Ireland.

British Library Cataloguing in Publication Data
A catalogue record for this book is available from the British Library.

ISBN 0-86327-762-4

10 9 8 7 6 5 4 3 2 1

Cover Illustration: Little Bird
Cover Design: Slick Fish Design, Dublin
Typesetting: Wolfhound Press
Printed in the UK by Cox & Wyman Ltd, Reading, Berks.

Chapter One

Michael Lynch knew they were watching him.

He stopped his Kawasaki motorcycle outside the Werburgh Street unemployment office and sat for a moment looking at the unmarked police car parked on the opposite side of the road. Inside the car, two plain-clothes policemen had their heads bent over a map, pretending they weren't watching him.

Michael grinned, got off the bike and leisurely walked into the building. He felt only contempt for the police, and he never let them worry him.

The Department of Social Welfare's office on Werburgh Street was a miserable-looking Victorian structure with high ceilings and barred windows. Inside the main ground-floor hall, queues of unemployed men waited to collect their weekly allowance, dull and bored.

The sudden appearance of Michael Lynch, standing in the doorway in his crash helmet, caused many of them to brighten and smile, nudging others to take a look at the man who had just arrived, followed by a buzz of whispering.

Michael Lynch was becoming a legend in his own town, and nearly every man in the hall claimed to possess some exclusive information about him. Most of the stories were clearly made up and totally untrue, but that was just a minor fact, to be ignored during the telling and listening and later repeating.

'H'lo, Michael, how're yeh?' one or two called out, as he manoeuvred through the queues to get to his own line.

As always, Michael responded with confidence and charm, and the brown eyes behind the mask were bright with smiling humour. He was a humorous man, a born joker who loved nothing more than making fun of the police and playing notorious pranks on them, making them look like hapless eejits, and laughing hilariously about it afterwards.

He was also reputed to be an audacious and dedicated criminal who had been responsible for a number of successful major robberies in the city, netting himself a personal fortune of over half a million.

But few men in the unemployment lines really believed that. Despite the sinister balaclava he often wore — which they claimed was nothing more than one of his jokes on the police — they simply would not believe it.

For one thing, they argued, *if* Michael Lynch had masterminded all those successful robberies — and that, mind, was a very big *IF* — then success had definitely not gone to his clothes. He still wore the same casual jeans and T-shirts and bomber jackets he had always worn. There had been no change in his style over the past few years, no change at all.

'Half a million!' they laughed. 'What lucky fucker with half a million lovely quid would bother to come down to this fuckin' dole office and queue up for a few paltry pounds of welfare every week?'

And that was what Michael Lynch did, every week without fail: queued and signed for his unemployment assistance at the Werburgh Street welfare office.

None of the clerks behind the counter believed it

either. All of them knew Michael Lynch well, and they were no longer intimidated or frightened by his ludicrous insistence on wearing a balaclava. The man clearly lived in a fantasy world of his own. But he was always pleasant and polite, and — unlike the rest of the gobshites who formed the daily queues — he never argued, never complained, and was always gently spoken.

Michael saw his friend Tony Brady at the top of the queue, slowly and hesitantly signing the docket. He slipped into the queue behind him and gave Tony a nudge.

Tony looked around. 'Ah, how're yeh, Michael? Long time no see.'

Michael grinned. 'Where would we be without the Social Welfare, eh?'

'Couldn't agree more, Michael. It's a vital few bob.'

Their conversation was solely for the benefit of the clerk behind the counter.

'The thing is,' Michael said seriously, 'what it means to our wives and kids.'

'Sure, I know.' Tony was now collecting his money, looking directly at the clerk with a tragic expression on his face. 'It's the difference between them eating or not eating sometimes.'

Michael nodded. 'You said it, pal.'

Tony turned to leave, still talking about the difficulty of life on the dole, while below the counter his hand took the motorbike keys that Michael slipped to him.

'Good luck,' Michael called, as Tony walked away.

Michael moved up to the window and smiled at the clerk. As always, his voice was extremely polite.

'Michael Lynch. And how are you today?'

The clerk was young and nervous and new to the job. This was his second week behind the counter, and the second time he had seen Michael Lynch — a man who proved that Dublin was now a place gone mad. Where else in the world could a man walk about in the broad daylight of a hot July afternoon wearing a black balaclava over his face?

Only today he wasn't wearing a balaclava, just his motorcycle helmet. It wasn't the latest style of Robocop-type helmet, but the type that left the eyes visible and had a leather strap covering the mouth.

The dark eyes visible under the helmet were smiling humorously at the clerk. He smiled nervously back, and asked the mandatory questions:

'Have you sought employment in the past week?'

'I'm always seeking employment.'

'Have you secured a regular job in the past week?'

'Sorry, no.'

'What kind of work are you seeking, Mr Lynch?'

'Oh, anything. But the job market for a man of thirty-nine is not exactly flourishing, is it? So what kind of job do *you* think I should seek?' Michael asked.

'I — I don't know.' The clerk, nonplussed, nervously looked down at his list as if searching for the next question.

Michael's dark eyes quickly looked towards the main doorway, where Stevie Brady was handing Tony a black leather jacket identical to the one Michael was wearing. Tony swiftly shrugged the jacket on; a second later he had also put on the crash helmet Stevie gave him.

And then Tony was gone.

*

'Here comes Lynch!'

The two detectives in the unmarked car jerked upright when Tony Brady came out of the dole office, head down, and walked towards the Kawasaki — looking like Michael to the life.

The driver spoke into the handset of his radio. 'Control, it's Unit 4. Michael Lynch has come out. He's getting on the bike.'

Control crackled back, *'Right, Unit 4, continue covert surveillance.'*

Tony kicked the bike into life and screeched off at speed.

The unmarked car sped after him. 'Okay, he's off on his travels, heading south, but we're up his hole, Control.'

From the doorway of the unemployment office, Stevie Brady watched the police car speeding after Tony, a huge grin on his face.

*

Michael had gathered up his money and was slowly and carefully counting it. He glanced towards the main door and saw Stevie give him the nod. He stopped counting. 'Yeah, it's all there, all correct.'

He folded the money and pushed it into the pocket of his jeans. 'You're a gentleman, do you know that?' he said to the clerk. 'Listen, now, I'm dead serious! It's conscientious and upright fellas like you that make this world go round.'

'Thank you, Mr Lynch.'

'Well, goodbye for now, and good luck. See you next week.' He smiled at the relieved clerk, and walked away.

Stevie was waiting for him outside the doorway. 'The police car's gone after Tony.'

Michael nodded. They fell into step and walked round the corner, to where another parked car was waiting.

Alec Duignan, a skilful twenty-year-old wheelsman,

saw them approach through his rear-view mirror. A second later Michael's younger brother, Billy Lynch, opened the passenger door and stepped out. Without a word, without fuss, but at speed, Billy handed each man a different jacket to wear and a balaclava.

Michael smiled at his brother. 'Good work, little fella.'

Billy moved quickly to the back of the car, opened the boot and took out two pump-action rifles. The two men took the guns, placed them under cover of their unzipped jackets and held them there, then turned and calmly walked back to the unemployment office.

They entered casually — then suddenly exploded into action, guns raised and pointing, shouting for everyone to lie flat on the floor. *'Come on, down! Get the fuck down!'*

The whole room collapsed like a punctured balloon. Both guns were now aimed at the clerks.

'Go ahead and raise the alarm — if you value the government's money more than your lives,' Michael shouted. 'One rapid burst from this rifle and the six of you'll be dead in six seconds. Want that?'

The clerks shook their heads and raised their hands in the air. 'No, no, no...'

Billy appeared, also hooded and armed, guarding the doorway.

Michael silently gestured to one of the terrified clerks, who instantly started to gather up money.

*

The afternoon sun streamed down onto the city streets as Tony Brady slowly wove his motorcycle through the traffic, making sure the unmarked police car didn't lose him.

'I'll say one thing for Lynch, he sticks to the speed limit.'

The two detectives in the car were getting pissed off, restless for some action. Both country lads, they had come to Dublin's fair city in the hope of rising to the heights of their profession, but this joyride was getting them nowhere.

The driver was Barry Kavanagh, well-built and tough. His partner was Con Maguire, also well-built and tough. They had a lot more in common — their mutual love of football, and their hatred of criminals. Barry and Con considered all criminals to be their personal enemies. As police officers, they were the law; and criminals were *against* the law.

Fifteen minutes later they were feeling even more pissed off, even more restless, as they cruised in traffic at fifteen miles an hour behind the Kawasaki.

Barry finally took a packet of mints from the dashboard, popped one in his mouth and began to suck it with despair. 'Wouldn't this make you feel sorry for poor oul' taxi-drivers?' he muttered. 'All that sitting in traffic, day in and day out. Enough to do your head in, wha'?'

Con nodded. 'Turn anyone's brain to mush.'

On the Kawasaki, Tony Brady glanced at his watch and suddenly shot forward at speed.

Barry hastily put the car into gear and slammed down on the accelerator.

'Oho, here we go!' Con shouted into the handset. 'He's off at full speed. Something's happening, Control.'

'You're telling me! We've just had a report of a robbery in Werburgh Street dole office.'

'Ah, fuck — what? A robbery? Will we go back there?'

'No, stick with Lynch.'

Chapter two

The gang's getaway car was speeding towards Rathmines. Alec Duignan was an expert wheelsman, always in full control.

In the front passenger seat, Michael held onto the dashboard as the car took another sharp turn. He had changed back into his leather jacket and was heading towards his alibi.

The car dropped speed and finally cruised to a halt outside the Rathmines Garda Station. Michael tossed his crash helmet back to Stevie and opened the door. 'Okay, lads, see you tomorrow.'

Alec Duignan's hands moved caressingly over the steering-wheel. He loved cars even more than he loved his fiancée, and he was always appreciative when a motor gave him a nice performance. 'Great work, sweetheart. Now let's you and me roll!'

The car rolled away as Michael strolled into the garda station. At the desk he took out his licence and insurance papers and offered them to the desk sergeant.

'I'm Michael Lynch.'

The sergeant snarled, 'I know who you are, Lynch,' but he still examined the licence and insurance.

'I want to make a complaint, Sergeant.'

'About what?'

'A barking dog.'

The sergeant gave him a sneering look; he knew his form. 'Who're you after robbing, Lynch?'

'Sorry?'

'You will be.'

'Listen, now, Sergeant, I think we're at cross purposes here. You see, it's the neighbour's, Sergeant. She's a right bitch. The dog. Something's gotta be done about her. She keeps me awake all night, you know!'

The sergeant took a long, deep breath to calm himself. 'Do you think we're fools, Lynch?'

Michael imitated the barking dog. *'Woof! Woof!* Real loud, you know, persistent...'

'I said, do you think we're all fools, Lynch?'

I think you're all stupid pricks, Michael thought.

'Not at all, Sergeant, not at all. But, you know, I do have a civil *right* to come here with my complaint. And another thing — I want it logged there in that book, my complaint. I want it logged. That's the rules, you know?'

The sergeant snapped the book across the desk and lifted his pen, growling out each word as he entered the date and time and — 'Michael Lynch! Complaint about a neighbour's barking dog! Anything else?'

'No, that's it,' Michael said, putting his licence and insurance papers back into his pocket and sneakily glancing at his watch. 'But my poor bladder is near to bursting. I'll have to nip into the toilet.'

*

Tony Brady cruised the Kawasaki to a stop outside the Rathmines Garda Station. The two detectives following in the unmarked car looked at each other, puzzled.

'What the hell is Lynch doing now?'

'Looks like he's going into the station — cheeky fuck.'

*

Head down, Tony Brady entered the station, bypassed the desk, and walked swiftly down the corridor into the toilets. His eyes flashed around the white-tiled room — no gardaí at the sinks or urinals.

He darted into the first cubicle and locked the door, then took off his crash helmet and threw it over the partition, into the next cubicle, followed by the motorcycle key.

Ten seconds later, Michael opened the door of the second cubicle and walked out, crash helmet on and keys in hand.

'The plan demands split-second timing,' Michael had instructed the men. 'I repeat: careful, split-second timing.'

*

The detectives sat alert when Michael came out of the garda station and mounted the Kawasaki.

'Control, Lynch has come out of the station now. What was that all about?'

'Desk sergeant says he was in to complain about a barking dog. Taking the mickey, as usual. Don't let him out of your sight, do you hear me?'

As soon as the Kawasaki moved off, the unmarked car followed.

'He's off, but we're still up his hole, Control.'

*

Tony Brady came out of the station grinning to himself. Luck had been on their side all the way today — but then, it usually was. It was all down to Michael, who always believed he would win in the end. His faith in his own expertise made him successful in everything he touched. His lack of guilt, and his gusto for life and living and rustling and hustling, made working with him a treat, a real pleasure.

Tony's affection for Michael ran deep. They had played together as children, and their friendship had never waned since. They had come out of the same gutter and robbed the same banks. Pals all the way.

There was very little about Michael Lynch that Tony Brady didn't know. And one thing he knew for certain: Michael feared no one. Not the gardaí, and not the IRA. He never let them get under his skin, never let them worry him. If anyone tried to muscle in on his game, or annoy him in any way, he just told them to go fuck themselves. Simple as that. No discussion.

But what Tony loved best was that Michael was a man you could trust with your life. He was a natural-born bandit whom everyone liked.

Tony saw a bus coming, but he let it pass and hailed a taxi instead. He could afford it. Judging by the wads of notes in the bags, the raid on the dole office had netted at least sixty grand.

He sat back in the taxi and looked out the window, still grinning. One other thing he knew about his pal Michael Lynch: he was fucking nuts. Tony was sure of it. Who else would dare to rob his own dole office?

*

The suburbs were less congested than the city streets, and there was a cool, light breeze in the late-afternoon sunshine.

Michael enjoyed every minute of the bike's fast skim towards his home. He handled the Kawasaki with panache and style. Motorcycles were one of his passions; the Kawasaki was his latest acquisition, and if it weren't for his participation in the robbery, he would never have allowed Tony Brady or anyone else to ride it.

Michael had four true personal passions in his life: motorbikes, robberies, his marriage to a wife he adored, and his love affair with her sister.

He turned the bike into his road and saw the family car approaching the house from the opposite direction. He pulled the bike up in front of the house, and the car stopped four feet in front of it. Christine and Lisa and the five children piled out.

The unmarked police car had parked on the corner at the top of the tree-lined road, half-hidden by the thick trunk and branches of one of the trees.

Con bent his head low and peered forward to get a better look. 'Is that them? Is that the two sisters?'

'Sure is.' Barry smirked. 'The family that lays together, stays together, hah?'

'Jayz, they're nice enough, though, both of them. I bet he was glad he didn't have to choose between them, wha'?'

Christine Lynch was in her thirties, dark and sultry and very attractive. Her younger sister Lisa was not so obviously good-looking, but she had a certain cheeky charm about her.

The five small children were jumping around Michael. He grinned at his wife, Christine.

'Sorry I'm late — bit of a hold-up.' He glanced in the direction of the unmarked garda car. 'And now I have to show someone around the town. Is that all right with you?'

Christine smiled. 'It's grand with me.' She handed him the car keys. 'See you tonight.'

Barry and Con stared as Michael gave Christine a hug and a kiss on the cheek, then turned and did the same to Lisa.

'Did you see that!' Con looked at Barry, outraged. 'Hugging and kissing both of them — in front of each other!'

Barry was now looking at the house, a large four-bedroomed detached house that was reputed to have cost Lynch a hundred grand a few years ago. God knows what it would cost now. Neither Con nor Barry could have afforded anything remotely similar to it on their salaries.

'And they say crime doesn't pay,' Barry muttered.

'Not in the end, it doesn't.'

'He's moving — looks like he's gonna get in the car.'

Michael got into the car, quickly dipped down below the dashboard for a few seconds, then popped up with the crash helmet off and his balaclava back up over his face.

Barry gripped the steering-wheel and snapped, 'Ah, give us a look at your face, ye fuck!'

Michael gave Lisa the crash helmet. 'There you go, sweetheart. You know what to do.'

Lisa nodded.

Michael grinned at the five kids standing by the car door. 'Behave yourselves, do you hear me? Do what your mothers tell you.'

'Bye, Da!' the kids shouted, as he started up the car and slowly pulled away. 'Bye, Da! Bye!'

'Jesus, where's he going now?' Barry gunned his own engine in readiness for pursuit.

'Control, Lynch is off on his travels again, but in a car this time.'

'Does he know you've been following him?'

'No, Control, I don't think so. We've kept ourselves hidden behind traffic or trees, and he's never once turned his head in our direction or looked around him or anything. I don't think he's twigged us at all.'

'Right, Unit 4, continue covert surveillance.'

*

Christine Lynch was, at thirty-four, an extremely attractive woman. She had green eyes, a small straight nose, full lips, and glossy black hair cut into a straight bob around her face. As a teenager, she had been a devastatingly pretty girl with a seductively husky voice — although she had only ever been seductive with one man, and she had later married him.

Her sister Lisa was six years younger, brown-haired, feisty, and quite pretty in a gamine way. She also knew how to calm Christine when her deepest fears threatened to overwhelm her.

Christine and Lisa were not only sisters and close friends, but also very protective of each other and their children. They kept their lives intensely private from the world outside, refusing to talk about their unique relationship with anyone.

'Because,' as Christine often advised Lisa, 'no one would ever understand.'

*

Dublin was far behind. The setting sun was casting a purplish-red glow over the dusky folds of the Wicklow Hills. Michael had been driving at a cruising speed for two hours, but he felt no boredom, no restlessness; he had always loved the peace and tranquillity of the green valleys and lonely hills of Wicklow.

A Van Morrison tape was playing on the car's stereo.

He tapped his fingers on the steering-wheel as he listened, his dark eyes occasionally glancing at the rear-view mirror. The unmarked garda car was still following behind... He smiled. Van Morrison sang on...

Behind the wheel of the unmarked garda car, Barry looked disgruntled as Con went over and over his puzzlement about Michael Lynch.

'So, like, okay, but tell me this — how can a man who owns an expensive house like that still go along to the unemployment office every week and collect free money off the State?'

'Because he's a cheeky fuck, that's why.'

'But surely —' Con twisted round in his seat and looked curiously at Barry. 'Surely the Welfare have asked questions and made enquiries and looked into all this?'

'They have, but Lynch has got them by the bollix. He claims the house belongs to his sister-in-law, not him. He's even got legal deeds to show the house is in her name — the Lisa one. He claims some rich old boyfriend, an English fella who finally went back home to his wife, bought it for her a few years ago — cash down and no mortgage.'

'So, like, where's *he* supposed to live, then?'

'Well, everyone knows he lives in the big house with his wife Christine and their children. But he's *supposed* to live in a smaller house the Corporation gave him years ago. Only he doesn't live there, the sister-in-law does.'

Con leaned over to the dashboard and took a Murray Mint from the pack. 'Jesus, I still can't make sense of it,' he said, his mouth bulging with the mint. 'So the big house is in the sister-in-law's name — only she doesn't live there. And the Corporation house is in Lynch's name — but he doesn't live there.'

Barry nodded. 'Lynch claims it was a straight swop,

because him and Christine have the larger family. All a scam, of course. Lynch bought the big house, no doubt about that. But *proving* it's the problem. See, I've read this fucker's file, and all this is part of Lynch's MO...'

Barry spun the wheel as he turned a sharp corner, then continued, 'You see, in everything he does, Lynch loves nothing more than fucking up people's heads so they don't know who's who, or what's what, or how or where.'

Con crunched on his mint and looked searchingly around through the car window. 'I wonder where we are now.'

'Fuckin' nowhere, by the looks of it. I thought you were supposed to be keeping your eye on the map. Oh, Jesus...' Barry's eyes were staring at the fuel gauge.

*

Michael turned his car up a narrow road that led into a remote part of the mountains, desolate and dense with ancient, tall pine trees darkening the sky, miles from anywhere.

Barry was talking worriedly to Control. 'Hello, listen — now we're up the Sally Gap, about five miles east of Lara and ten from Bray.'

'You're where? You mean he hasn't —'

'He's been driving non-stop. We think he must have arranged to meet someone out here. But we're getting very low on petrol. Where's the nearest service station?'

'Jesus... Right, be back to you in a minute.'

Up ahead, Michael Lynch's car drew to a halt by some trees. Barry put his foot down on the brake.

'Hold on — hold on, Control. This is it now! Here we go! Lynch is getting out of the car.'

It was only when Michael Lynch opened the boot of his car and took out the five-gallon petrol drum that Barry and Con finally realised what game he had been playing.

'Ah, for fuck's sake!' Barry groaned. 'He's been playing us for a right pair of eejits all along!'

Both stared in humiliated horror as Michael Lynch finished refuelling his car, then turned and cheerily waved the empty drum at them.

'Control!... Hello... Hello... Ah, quick, Control... Hello!'

Control came back to them. *'Okay, lads, now your nearest service station is a good ten miles away, maybe more. North-east on the Bray road. So if you're facing Lara now, you have to turn back and go towards Brittas until you hit the coast road. Then turn left for Bray and there's an Esso on the left, three miles outside the town. But you'll have to move fairly fast, because it closes at nine o'clock...'*

They watched Michael Lynch get back into his car and drive away, leaving them in near-darkness, surrounded by lonely hills.

'Ten miles... Have we enough juice to get there, Barry?'

Barry slumped his head miserably over the wheel. 'No fuckin' chance. It's reading empty. And if Headquarters have to send a car all the way out here to rescue us, we're going to look a right pair of prats.'

* * *

Michael Lynch grinned as he drove at speed towards Dublin. He put another Van Morrison tape in the stereo. A nice long drive out to the country hills, music playing all around him, a police escort to make sure he didn't get lost... What a grand way to spend an evening.

Chapter three

Born into poverty and hunger in the slum flats of Dublin, Michael Lynch had begun his career as a thief when he was only nine years old. By then he had decided that the authorities didn't give a damn about anyone but themselves and the rich people. The police were their servants, helping the State to crush, kick and evict his neighbours. And so began his unrelenting war against them. He placed himself squarely on the opposite side of the road to the men in blue, and became a devout young criminal.

He had started his career at the very bottom — shoplifting. He didn't consider it a crime, but a necessity. If he hadn't stolen it, there would never have been enough food on the table. The shops could afford it, he had reasoned, and his mother was always grateful to him.

Although she had *tried* very hard, at times, to be furious with him, telling him stealing was wrong; but the money Michael's father earned from his porter's job was only a pittance — half of which he spent on drink in the pub, every Friday night, to try and blot out the failure of his life — and the rest was certainly not enough to pay the rent and feed and clothe a family of five children. So any food Michael brought into the house had been truly appreciated.

Michael had often sat looking at his father. *He's honest, and he's hungry,* he had thought. *I'm not going to end up like him — no way.*

Whenever he had seen his father scraping around in the rubbish bin in the kitchen, trying to find a spare bit of tobacco on a dead cigarette butt, desperate for a smoke, Michael had vowed, *I'll never smoke.* Food was essential to life; cigarettes were not.

And whenever he had watched his father stumbling home drunk on a Friday night, happy and singing and full of the joy of life, then as quiet and white-faced as a depressed skeleton the following morning, Michael had vowed, *I'll never drink alcohol.*

But, in those early-childhood years, Michael had developed his own cravings: sweets and lemonade and delicious cream cakes — luxuries to be dreamed of, which he had no money to afford.

It was a problem Michael learned to deal with. Whenever he craved sweets or a delicious cream cake in a shop, he just nicked them — and expertly, so he was never suspected or caught.

His father was honest and hungry, but he was not, and never would be.

In his teenage years, he had moved several steps up the ladder of his profession and become a burglar, choosing houses in the richer districts of the city and slipping in at night like a ghost. He had loved every minute of it, seeing himself in his own mind as some great avenger of the poor, a modern-day Dick Turpin in a mask, or a Robin-Hood figure collecting the loot and sharing it out with his friends.

Fair was fair, Michael had reasoned; how else were he and his friends going to get the money to pay for their food and fun? How else were they going to get the funds to see the latest film, or take a girl for a 7-Up and some ice-cream? They were all from the slums, all poorly educated, and the only jobs available for lads like them were tuppenny jobs that paid a pittance. No poor lad could ever develop into a happy man on a wage that small. No way!

Although — and Michael always insisted upon qualifying this point whenever it was raised — he might have been 'poorly educated' in an academic sense, he believed himself to be extremely intelligent and *clever-minded*. Almost a genius, in fact.

And, as the years went by, he proved that to be so, by masterminding a number of ingenious robberies that brought him in a small fortune.

But that was not enough for Michael Lynch. It was a *large* fortune he was after. One in excess of fifty million pounds was his ambition. Enough to keep him safe and allow him to end his days free from the fear of poverty.

Yes, fifty million was a fair target for a man of his talent and genius, he often reckoned. So, despite his successes so far, he still had a long way to go to achieve his goal.

But no matter what he did, or how he did it — even when things went wrong — he always kept on smiling. It was his biggest defence against the world, and his smile had become one of his trademarks. Not even his balaclava could hide that famous grin, and the police detested it.

One day, the gardaí vowed, they would knock that grin off Michael Lynch's face and lock him up in prison for the rest of his life.

*

Christine was upstairs, trying to get the kids into bed, when Michael arrived home from his evening drive around Wicklow.

Michael went straight into the kitchen and poured himself a glass of water. He pulled off his balaclava and drank the water in one long gulp.

At first sight, without hood or crash helmet, Michael Lynch was very ordinary. He was tall and well-built, with tightly cropped black hair, a style he had liked even before it became fashionable.

But it was his eyes that held the true sparkle and potency of his personality. When he smiled with his eyes, many women thought him extremely attractive, and at least two found him very sexy. He had a physical attraction that came and went with his mood or his situation. Like a chameleon, he could brighten up and be the life and soul of the party, then simply fade away into the shadows when he wanted to.

But there was a relentless strength about him that men liked, an unshakeable belief in his own talent and genius. He was a natural-born leader who loved life, loved a laugh, loved his two women, and also loved his gang.

For his friends, Michael Lynch would bend rules, break laws, and give any help he could. All he ever asked in return was true loyalty. He couldn't bear to spend time near any man or woman he couldn't trust. He was a complex man, a dreamer and a realist, ready to calculate the dangers and take enormous risks even when the odds were stacked against him.

Michael looked around the kitchen of his home. It was a beautiful home, designed on an open plan from one room to the next, with expensive stripped-pine wooden floors. He had spent thirty thousand pounds in cash to have it tastefully decorated and furnished. The kitchen had every mod. con. and a picture window looking out on the back garden. The huge living-room had a collection of plump white sofas and a large television with all the cable channels.

He had no regrets. He robbed banks, but he had never harmed anyone. His stick-ups had always been precisely planned and carried out with the minimum of fuss, and no one had ever got hurt.

He had escaped the gutter and become an ordinary decent criminal. He truly believed that he was ordinary and decent. His crimes were against the establishment and the powerhouses. The real criminals, in his view, were child abusers and drug dealers. They destroyed innocence, destroyed lives, left drugged-up teenagers laid out on mortuary slabs, and didn't care a toss about it.

They were the real criminals, and he despised them.

So, yes, he had escaped the gutter and become a bank robber. It had been the only route open to him.

All he wanted was what everyone else wanted: to be rich, to own a fortune, to be free of the fear of poverty. And, as somebody famous in history had once said, *Behind every great fortune there is a crime.*

He poured himself another glass of water. The pots and plates from the evening meal were piled around the sink, waiting to be scraped clean and put into the dishwasher. His eyes moved over the remains on the plates — bits of meat and vegetables and some good wholesome salad. Despite Christine's relentless efforts, all the kids had left the salad untouched; they always did. But they had still been well fed, and that was enough to fill Michael with satisfaction.

When Christine entered the kitchen, Michael glanced quickly at his watch and smiled at her. 'I just popped in to say hello.'

'Janey, now, amn't I honoured! Just a quick look in to say hello, is it?' She smiled warmly, to show she was joking.

Ever since their teenage years, Michael had always

thought Christine's smile to be just lovely. And, as the years passed, he also loved the way her figure slowly lost its youthful thinness and took on fuller curves in all the right places, like a lovely flower in full bloom.

He slipped his arms around her waist. 'Give us a kiss good night, anyway. Then I have to be going.'

'Are you staying at Lisa's tonight?'

'No, I have this court case tomorrow, remember? So I'll be staying at Stevie's tonight.'

Christine looked worried. 'Do you think they'll get the court to rescind your bail?' She bit her lip. 'I'm frightened, Michael. The guards are determined to get you locked up behind bars.'

'The guards — that bunch of Mickey Mouses!' He squared his shoulders confidently. 'They'll never beat me.'

'What time is the hearing?'

'Ten o'clock.' Michael grinned. 'But I have a little job to do before that.'

*

Next morning, Michael and Tony Brady, both hooded, checked their watches. It was exactly nine o'clock when they approached the locked door of the quiet bank.

An elderly man stood outside, waiting for the bank to open. He blanched at the sight of two balaclava'd men approaching him.

Both men smiled at him. 'How's it going?' Michael asked, in the friendly tone of people finding themselves in a queue.

The man seemed incapable of speech for a second, then stuttered out nervously, 'Oh, g-great ... ah — lovely day.'

Michael glanced at his watch again. 'These banks, they never open on time, do they?'

'No, no,' the man agreed. 'They're desperate, sure. Desperate, desperate altogether.'

Someone inside was unlocking the bank's door. Michael pulled a gun out and pointed it at the man. 'Try another branch.'

The man ran.

The door opened. The girl's happy morning face abruptly changed as Michael and Tony pushed her back inside.

'Morning,' Michael smiled, pointing his gun at her. 'A withdrawal, please.'

*

Like every other driver, Stevie Brady hated traffic, but this morning he was glad it could be relied upon. He was driving Michael's car, and the route and timing had been carefully planned the previous night.

Every few seconds Stevie glanced up at the rear-view mirror; he was approaching the meeting-point. If a delay occurred, he would just have to drive on slowly to the second point and hope they would catch up with him there.

'Ah, good lads!' he suddenly whispered. The Kawasaki was gently weaving its way through the traffic behind him. Tony was driving, and Michael was sitting pillion behind him; both were wearing crash helmets.

The motorcycle drew up alongside as the car came to a stop at traffic lights. Stevie waited until just before the lights were ready to turn green, then quickly opened the driver's door and moved over to the passenger seat.

Michael jumped off the bike and into the car as Tony sped off on the Kawasaki. He dumped the full bag onto Stevie's lap, whipped off his crash helmet, took the wheel and began driving towards the Bridewell.

'Nice timing,' Stevie grinned. 'Everything go okay?'

'Perfect.'

Michael turned the car out of the traffic and drove through a series of side-streets, stopping at a corner.

'See yeh,' Stevie said, grabbing up the bag.

'Hold on.' Michael reached for the bag, unzipped it and pulled out a wad of notes. 'Legal expenses,' he grinned.

Stevie didn't like Michael doing this. 'Jayz, you could write him a cheque, couldn't you?'

'Nah.' Michael stuffed the wad of notes into his pocket. 'Lawyers always insist on their backhanders in cash. Keeps it off the record, see?'

Stevie zipped up the bag and quickly got out of the car. Michael sat for a few seconds, watching him walk away and disappear down another side-street; then he turned the car around and drove at a relaxed speed towards the Four Courts.

*

The morning sun was shining brightly on the murky green water of the River Liffey as the car cruised along the quay and drew to a halt a few yards away from the courthouse.

Michael's solicitor, Brian Carroll, was standing outside, waiting for him. He moved quickly and slipped into the passenger seat of the car.

'Now listen, Michael,' he said, 'Harrison will defend the bail application, maybe even take the trial, but he insists on a private payment.'

'Yeah, you said.'

'Two thousand pounds in cash.'

'Two fucking grand!' Michael was shocked at the amount. 'For a morning's work?'

'Up front,' Brian said. 'As in now, before we go in.'

'The bollix! You mean he doesn't *trust* me?'

'Here he is, Michael. He's worth it. Come on.'

They got out of the car as the barrister, Fergus Harrison, approached them in white wig and black gown. He was a tall, thin-faced man in his fifties who specialised in criminal law. He knew every loophole, every flaw in the book that could be used to his advantage. But for the benefit of this knowledge and skill, he expected his clients to pay him a significantly greater sum of money than his clerk billed.

'Morning. It's nearly time,' Harrison said brightly, then added in a low aside, 'Are we in funds?'

'You mean the cash?' Michael asked loudly. 'I'll give it to you right here and now, I don't mind.' He moved to take the money from his pocket, enjoying the horrified reaction.

'No, no, no,' Harrison hissed. 'Not here, Mr Lynch!' He grabbed Michael's elbow. 'Come with me — and you *will* be taking that balaclava off in the courtroom, won't you?'

*

In Merrion Square, a long queue had formed at the entrance door of the National Gallery. After all the fuss and publicity, it seemed the whole of Ireland wanted to see the Caravaggio Exhibition.

Christine took her place in the queue.

She relished getting away on her own for a few hours and doing her own thing. Even as a child, she had always enjoyed drawing, and now she was loving her art classes at night school.

But you didn't have to like art to want to see the Caravaggio Exhibition. The whole country was talking about it. Caravaggio had been one of the greatest Italian masters of his time, and in 1610, in Italy, his religious masterpiece *The Taking of Christ* had gone missing. It had been lost to the art world for over three hundred years — until a year ago, when it had miraculously been discovered in a house in Dublin, of all places.

Art experts had verified that it was the original, painted by Caravaggio himself, a true treasure, worth in excess of thirty million pounds.

A treasure that now belonged to Ireland. A treasure that was ready to be exhibited to the world.

Half an hour later, Christine was inside the gallery and entering the large, airy room that housed the masterpiece. The white walls were pristine, the only colour coming from the paintings on the walls — all Caravaggio originals that had been brought in from museums all over Europe.

Christine stood before *The Taking of Christ* and stared at it for a very long time. Jesus in the garden, receiving the kiss of Judas the betrayer. His expression of resigned helplessness — surrounded by soldiers, and no chance of escape — moved her deeply.

She suddenly thought of her husband, poor Michael, surrounded by police in court, and wondered if he too was about to lose his freedom.

Chapter four

His payment pocketed, Fergus Harrison went on to give a grand performance in court.

'... The prosecution's claim that they fear my client might flee the jurisdiction while on bail has no foundation. Mr Lynch has never, ever left this country. He doesn't even hold a passport...'

The judge, a formidably pious and stern man, frowned as he looked directly at Harrison's client. Although they kept the judge in a job, he really had no time for criminals of any sort, and he looked down on them all with majestic contempt.

Michael sat listening, his head lowered and a hand covering his face, as Harrison continued in fine, sincere form, touching upon a subject that might soften the judge's heart.

'It is not an exaggeration to suggest that it would *break his heart* to leave his beloved Dublin. Especially when — if I may remind your Honour — Mr Lynch's lovely little daughter Breda will be making her First Holy Communion very soon.'

'First Holy Communion?'

The judge, a devout Catholic, approved of any father who instructed his children in the practice of the Sacraments.

'Yes, your Honour, her First Holy Communion. And surely it would be tragic if her father could not be with her on that very special day.'

Michael glanced up; the judge was clearly impressed by this point.

'The State,' Harrison continued with passion, 'can offer no cause, in law or in justice, why this quiet, unassuming, clean-living teetotaller should have his bail rescinded...'

*

'Here he comes!'

The waiting news media were in a frenzy, cameramen and journalists tumbling over one another in the sudden surge forward.

Michael, his balaclava back on, was the first out of the court building, followed by his barrister and solicitor. Microphones were shoved towards him.

'How does it feel to be the most wanted man in Ireland?'

'Why do you hide your face if you're innocent?'

'You enjoy making the gardaí look thick, don't you?'

Michael paused. His eyes were not on the journalists, but on the two detectives at the bottom of the steps. *Ah, so you finally got back from Wicklow!* he thought.

Barry Kavanagh and Con Maguire were glaring furiously at him.

Michael turned a humorous grin to the journalists. 'Hold on now a minute, lads, hold on till I tell you. Don't ever think the gardaí are thick, because that'd be a big mistake. You'd be wrong. The gardaí are anything but thick.'

Some of the cameramen and journalists chuckled.

'No, no, I'm serious now... In fact, I think the gardaí are very, very clever.'

He moved to walk on; the media followed him. At the

bottom of the steps, Barry and Con barred his path.

Barry was still glaring. 'Are you Michael Lynch?'

Michael turned to the journalists. 'See what I mean — *brains*, you see?'

'Michael Lynch,' Barry said authoritatively, 'I am detaining you on suspicion of possessing illegal substances under the Misuse of Drugs Act.'

'What?'

Brian Carroll stepped forward. 'Excuse me, I am Mr Lynch's solicitor, and anything you —'

But Barry and Con had already grabbed Michael.

'Now *hold on*!' Brian Carroll exclaimed.

A document was shoved in his face. 'Here's the warrant!' Con said.

Michael had begun to struggle. 'I know what yous want — you want to strip-search me, don't you? Yous dirty perverts!'

'Come on, Lynch —'

'You think you'll humble me, don't you?'

'You're under arrest!' Barry snapped.

'You can go as low as you like,' Michael said, 'but I'll go lower.'

He began to pull at his own clothes, stripping off his leather jacket, pulling his T-shirt over his head.

The two detectives couldn't understand what he was doing. They looked at each other in baffled confusion. The photographers moved in. Barry and Con desperately began to try and stop Michael taking any more of his clothes off.

'Do you see what they do to innocent people?' Michael called to the journalists, his trousers now off. 'Dirty perverts getting their rocks off. Trying to get a feel. This is what I have to put up with. Jesus! — Did you see that? Did you see him trying to grab my balls?'

The two detectives were backing off. The journalists were all laughing.

'Look! Drugs? Where are the drugs? I've never had drugs in me life, and everyone knows it. Come on, you two square-heads — come over and shove your hand up me arse...' He pulled down his shorts. 'Come on, find some drugs.'

The cameras were clicking and flashing in a frenzy.

Barry and Con could take no more, fearful of what Lynch would do or say next.

The crowd of onlookers cheered and jeered as the two detectives backed off quickly and got into the unmarked car, driving away at speed.

Michael relaxed and grinned.

*

The front page of the *Evening Herald* carried a photograph of Michael Lynch, masked, and a huge headline: *CRIME BOSS REVEALS EVERYTHING — EXCEPT HIS FACE.*

Christine stood in the kitchen, staring at the photograph. She looked over at Michael, a hint of a smile on her face.

Michael was serenely eating his dinner. Three of his children, Tommy, Shane and Breda, were sitting at the table with him.

'Do you want any more, love?' Christine asked.

'No, that was grand.' Michael looked up hopefully. 'Unless there's dessert.'

'Of course there is.'

While his mother turned away to get the dessert, Tommy, a sparky eight-year-old, pointed to a piece of steak left on Michael's plate and quickly whispered, 'Da, can I finish that?'

'Course you can,' Michael whispered back. 'Waste not, want not.' He forked the meat onto Tommy's plate.

Christine returned to the table, carrying a tray of lemonade and cream cakes. Her face fell when she saw Tommy eating the steak. 'Ah, Michael, you didn't give him some of your meat, did you? You know the way red meat makes him hyper!'

'Sorry — sorry, wasn't thinking.'

Christine frowned at Tommy. 'You just better go to bed when you're told tonight, do you hear? And no giddy-acting.'

She placed the cakes on the table, and all the children grabbed at them. 'Ah, ah, ah — your father first,' Christine said sternly. 'Who earns the money in the house?'

A bored chorus. 'Da does.'

'Ah, sure, they're a grand bunch o' kids.' Michael lifted a cake from the plate. 'And there's loads for everyone.'

'No, Michael, they have to learn. Oh, wait now — I have something to show you...'

Christine disappeared out to the hall and came back unrolling a poster. 'Look, Michael, d'you see this?'

Michael stared at the poster. 'What is it?'

'It's a painting, of course — a print of a painting.'

'I can see that, but what is it?'

'It's called *The Taking of Christ*. I bought it in the National Gallery. Do you mind if I hang it up in our bedroom?'

Michael made a face. The picture was a bit grim — not the sort of thing you'd want in your bedroom; but then, Christine's taste in pictures had gone a bit weird since she'd begun her part-time course in art.

'A holy picture. What do you want a holy picture for?'

'I knew you'd say that. It's not a holy picture. It's a Caravaggio. He was about as holy as you are.'

Michael shrugged. 'Looks like a holy picture to me.'

'Can I hang it up, or can't I?'

'Of course you can.'

'And you won't be slagging me about it, will you?'

Michael smiled at her. 'No, I promise.'

She looked delighted. 'Oh, grand.' She disappeared out the door to hang it straight away.

Michael winked at Tommy. 'Women, hah?'

*

A glorious summer sunset reddened the sky. Michael and Tommy were kneeling by an upturned bicycle in the back garden, fixing a puncture.

Tommy looked at his father with his wide child's eyes. 'Why does it keep happening, Da?'

'Because you don't watch where you're going. You see, every time you go out on the road there's dangers out there. Bits of glass lying in wait, nails, thumbtacks, potholes. So you have to watch out — watch your every move. Because if you don't, they'll get you.'

'Who?'

'The bits of glass and that — sooner or later, if you're not careful. And then you get a puncture. And then you're fucked.'

'And then you fix it for me,' Tommy said.

'Yeah, I do.' Michael grinned. 'Aren't you a clever little shite.'

Tommy nodded. 'Can I put the patch on?'

'Yeah, but don't wrinkle it... There you go. You've done it. If a job's worth doing...?'

Tommy shrugged. 'I can't remember.'

'It's worth doing well. Say it now.'

'It's worth doing well.'

'Say it all again, to remember it.'

Tommy rattled it off. 'If a job's worth doing, then it's worth doing well.'

'That's it. Come on, let's pump this thing up; let's see have we got you on the road again.'

*

Shortly after midnight, Michael wheeled the bicycle out to the dark and deserted street and threw his leg over it. He cycled off, waving back at Christine framed in the doorway.

'Night, love,' she called. 'See you tomorrow.'

Chapter five

All the windows were in darkness when Michael arrived at Lisa's house in Rathmines. He took out his keys, opened the door, and quietly wheeled the bike inside.

He stood in the hall and looked upwards. A dim light shone onto the landing through the bathroom door, which was always left ajar at night for the kids.

He crept up the stairs and into the back bedroom, where his two children were sound asleep. He bent over the beds and softly kissed each child in the darkness.

Lisa was just a mound under the duvet when he slipped into their bedroom. He took off his jacket and draped it on the back of a chair.

'Michael...?' Lisa's head emerged. 'That you?'

'Go back to sleep if you want.'

She pushed down the duvet and turned to him. 'No, I'm awake now.'

He bent down and kissed her. 'Sorry I'm late. I was watching telly with Christine. Your man, Jerry Springer. That show's all about sex and nothing else.'

'Sex?' Lisa smiled and stretched. 'Oh, so you'll be feeling horny now, I suppose?'

'Any minute now I will. Soon as I get in beside you.'

He sat down on the side of the bed and started to take off his shoes. 'Oh, yeah — what was it I had to tell you? Christine said she forgot to ask you earlier. Will you mind Tommy and Shane tomorrow afternoon? She has to go into town to get Breda her First Communion dress.'

'I will, no problem.'

'Thanks.'

He took off the rest of his clothes and got in beside Lisa, pulling her close and feeling her warmth, kissing her mouth and hugging her. They started to make love, slow and smoochy.

Suddenly there was a terrific hammering on the front door.

'Jee-sus!' Michael did a quick roll out of bed and went to the window. He pulled back the curtain slightly and looked down: a squad car was outside, with two detectives in the back seat. Barry Kavanagh and Con Maguire were standing at the front door, looking up at the window.

'It's the fucking Mickey-Mouse brigade.'

The hammering came again.

'Fuck 'em!' Lisa said frustratedly. 'Don't answer.'

'Nah, I'll have to.' Michael moved to the chair and started to get dressed.

'Come on, Lynch,' Barry Kavanagh shouted up. 'We have a warrant to bring you in for questioning. Commissioner Daly's orders.'

Michael frowned. *Commissioner Daly?*

He turned to Lisa. 'Ring Billy, will you? Tell him what's happened.'

He shrugged on his jacket. 'Tell him the gardaí are beginning to push me too far. Tell him to ring round the boys and get the job done on the golf course tonight — and I mean *tonight*. I want tomorrow cancelled.'

'What d'you mean?' Lisa asked, puzzled.

'Just do as I say.' Michael smiled vengefully in the darkness. 'Billy and the others know the plan.'

*

In the interrogation room at the Central Detective Unit, Michael sat in a pool of dim light, silent and calm.

From the very start, he had made it clear to his interrogators that he would not be answering any of their questions. He had then folded his arms, sat back, and seemed content to gaze blankly at a spot on the wall above the detectives' heads.

Barry and Con were sure they could break him. They sat side by side on two chairs behind a table, going through the old routine like a double act.

Con: Where did you stay last night? Was it Stevie Brady's house?

Barry: It was Stevie's house, all right.

Con: 33 St Dympna's Gardens. Stevie and his eight kids.

Barry: Slept on the floor, did you?

Con: Very uncomfortable.

Barry: Handy for the bank, though.

Con: Yeah, it was handy for the bank, wasn't it?

Barry: We know how you worked it. From the bank to the court.

Con: We do, you know.

Barry: We have witnesses. They saw the switch.

Con: So come on, Lynch. We'll tell you. All you have to say is, 'Yes, that's the way it was.'

Detective Sergeant Noel Quigley entered the interrogation room. He sat down on a chair in a shadowed corner of the room, and listened.

Quigley noticed that Michael Lynch hadn't so much as batted an eyelid when he entered. His stare was fixed on some spot on the wall; his mind seemed to be miles away from the scene around him. Nothing the two detectives said had produced any kind of reaction from Lynch, any reaction whatever.

Barry: Who was with you at the bank?
Con: It was Stevie. No, did Stevie drive the car?
Barry: Stevie drove the car, right? Tony Brady was in the bank with you, yeah?

*

Eventually, every man meets his match. And Detective Sergeant Noel Quigley felt very confident that he would prove to be more than a match for a scumbag like Michael Lynch.

A tall, lean-framed man in his early forties, with dark hair and even darker eyes, born and brought up in County Meath, Noel Quigley had cleverly bested colleagues in the cutthroat rivalry for promotion and had risen through the ranks of the gardaí to become a senior policeman.

And now he had been given a new case to deal with, a new criminal to hound, catch, charge and prosecute and lock up for good: the king of the Dublin underworld himself — Michael Lynch.

Barry: We have witnesses, Lynch.
Con: You came to court on the motorbike and switched at the last minute, right?
Barry: Fifteen minutes — easy on a motorbike.
Con: Give us an answer!

Noel Quigley's eyes were fixed on Michael Lynch. His

stare was still focused on the wall. Never once had he so much as glanced at the two detectives questioning him.

Quigley was intrigued. In his experience, most criminals usually hid behind smart remarks and a tough exterior, but Lynch looked like he just couldn't be bothered. He sat with an unusual stillness, calm and careless, although now his expression was showing hints of being truly bored.

Barry: All right, all right. We'll start all over again. You didn't sleep with either of your 'wives' on Monday night. We know that much.

Noel Quigley casually interrupted.

'So, Michael, if you weren't with the two ugly sisters — don't tell us you were off banging some other slag?'

Michael flicked an eye at him, briefly, furiously — then looked away again, his expression conveying the same old nothing.

But Noel Quigley was smirking, because he had at least got a reaction.

*

It was almost 9.00 a.m. when the desk sergeant unlocked the cell door. 'Okay, Lynch, you can go.'

Michael was stretched out on the pallet. He had been in a deep sleep. He sat up and blinked. 'What time is it?'

'Nine o'clock.'

'So what's for breakfast? Oh — did I tell you I like my rashers grilled crispy? And the egg not too —'

'Fuck off, Lynch.'

Michael stood up, sighed, flexed his shoulders and massaged the back of his neck.

The desk sergeant snapped, 'Detective Kavanagh is waiting to sign you out, so come on.'

Michael gave him a smile, then left the cell.

Barry Kavanagh was in a foul mood. Not only had the night's operation proved a complete waste of time, but now Commissioner Daly was on the phone to Detective Sergeant Quigley, ranting and raging at him, in a right state.

Noel Quigley was speaking into the desk sergeant's phone when Barry led Michael into the lobby.

'Well, no, but the order to bring Lynch in came down from yourself, sir... No, I'm not saying —'

'What's up?' Michael looked at Barry, his expression sympathetic. 'Something wrong, eh?'

Barry sniffed, certain he was getting flu. 'Some cheeky young fucks have vandalised the golf course.'

'Oh.'

'I hate this city,' Barry said.

'Yeah. Know what you mean.' Michael's voice was full of sympathy and understanding. Barry was surprised, turned and looked at him, saw the grin, and knew Lynch was faking it.

'I mean,' said Michael, 'an ordinary decent man is denied a night's sleep, and a load of top brass in the gardaí are denied a day's golf. And all for no reason at all. But that's this city. Only in Dublin...' He grinned again.

And Barry suddenly knew that Lynch had done it, organised the assault on the golf course. He went bug-eyed, his mouth open, his mind trying to work out *how*.

'Well,' Michael said cheerfully, 'at least yous won't be blaming me for it. Because I was held here in custody all night, wasn't I?'

He walked away grinning.

*

The destruction was beyond belief.

Commissioner Daly stood on the eighteenth green of the golf course, his mobile phone to his ear as he stared at the ruin all around him.

'There's a hole here the size of a lake!' he roared. 'And as deep — at least ten feet! This wasn't done by kids! Only a JCB could dig out a hole that big. Whoever it was must have *driven* a JCB onto the green!'

Downright sacrilege. Daly could hardly contain himself.

'The green is decimated! Listen, Quigley, this is —'

Daly was interrupted by the crowd of angry golfers demanding some kind of explanation for this mischief. 'Was it the IRA?'

'No.'

Daly was sure it was not the IRA, nor any other political group. No, this was some kind of prank, a well-planned bad joke, a deliberate mockery of the gardaí and a savage sabotage of a very special day.

'Listen, Quigley,' Daly roared into his mobile, 'I know you're not a golfing man, but the Association of Inspectors and Superintendents' Annual Golf Match has had to be cancelled — *cancelled*!'

At the other end of the line, Detective Sergeant Noel Quigley knew without any doubt that Michael Lynch was somehow responsible for the assault on the golf course; but he also knew he would never be able to prove it.

'Bastard,' he whispered. He stood, trapped and angry, as Commissioner Daly continued ranting down the phone at him about the cancellation of the day.

*

Outside the station, Lisa was sitting behind the wheel of her car, waiting. She smiled and opened the door for him.

'All right, Michael?'

'Fine.'

Lisa knew the routine, and so she had known what time to collect him. Whenever they pulled him in for questioning, they always kept him overnight and released him at nine o'clock the next morning.

As they drove away, Michael looked up at the clear blue sky and said thoughtfully, 'D'you know what? It's a lovely day for a game of golf.'

Lisa glanced at him. 'Did you say *golf*, Michael?'

'I did, Lisa.'

'Isn't that weird?'

'Why so?'

Lisa nodded to the car radio. 'I was just listening to the news there, and they were saying some golf course was attacked and destroyed last night for no reason at all. The gardaí are baffled. Imagine.'

'Like you say, weird.'

Michael suddenly let himself go. He had a laughing fit. He rolled his head on the back of the car seat and revelled in the sheer fun and triumph of it. He could see Commissioner Daly's face, all blown out and purple with fury.

'Ah, Daly,' he said, still laughing. 'That bastard put me in prison twice, when I was sixteen and again when I was eighteen. And all I did to him in return was spoil his day of golf.'

He cocked an eye at Lisa and said, with great good humour, 'That's my problem, you see. I have too good a heart.'

Chapter Six

Christine was reading her horoscope. It predicted a successful day that might turn out badly.

'I don't know why I read them,' she said to herself. 'It's all rubbish.'

She flicked over the page of her magazine to a new diet that guaranteed you maximum weight loss while still letting you eat as much as you liked. All you had to do was send off for special 'slimming soups' that worked like a miracle.

She grimaced in disgust as she looked at the exorbitant price of the soups. It was all such a con. All that slimmed was your wallet. Thank God she had never put on too much weight.

Breda came and stood by the table. 'Are we going into town?'

'Sure we are! Isn't that why you're having the day off school?'

Breda's little face was beaming rosily with delight. 'To get my First Holy Communion dress?'

'And *what* a dress it'll be!' Christine flung down the magazine and scooped her daughter onto her lap. 'And we'll have fizzy lemonade and cream cakes in Bewley's and make a real treat of it.'

*

They spent the afternoon in town, searching for a First Communion dress. It had to be beautiful, and the cost was no object, so it should have been easier than it turned out to be.

They left all the smaller shops, and most of the larger stores, feeling very disappointed. All polyester rubbish pretending to be silk, and nothing with any real style.

In O'Connell Street they went into Eason's bookstore, where Christine bought a beautifully illustrated book about Caravaggio and his work.

Breda was beginning to drag her feet and look sulky. They still hadn't found her new dress or had any lemonade and cakes in Bewley's.

But then, finally, in Brown Thomas's classy department store on Grafton Street, they found the perfect dress — an exquisite confection of white lace and frills, handmade in Italy. It looked stunning against Breda's dark, curly hair.

The assistant carefully placed the folded dress inside a white box and covered it with crispy white tissue paper.

On the bus home, Christine sat with the box on her lap. She was feeling very pleased with her purchase.

'Course, you know,' she said musingly to Breda, 'the Italians are very big on First Communions and lovely grand weddings. All the trimmings, and loads of fuss, and no expense spared. You could see that in the film *The Godfather*.'

Breda was looking out the bus window. She turned her face to her mother, puzzled. 'I thought it was only when you got baptised that you got a godfather.'

'It is, but what I meant was...' Christine smiled warmly at her daughter, then laughed. 'Ah, sure, you're only seven, what do you know?'

*

Later that night, Christine wandered into the living-room. She was in her bathrobe, drying her long hair with a towel. She looked at the clock — it was almost eleven.

Michael was settled in front of the television, very relaxed.

'Michael,' she said, 'the boys are still awake. They're saying you promised to tell them a story.'

'No way.'

'Well, go and sort it out, will you? They're sitting up in bed waiting for you.'

'The little chancers.' Michael reached for the remote and flicked off the TV.

Up in the bedroom, he found Tommy and Shane sitting in their beds, waiting.

'I never promised to tell you a story.'

'You did,' said Tommy. 'You did so, Da.'

'Now what did I tell you about lying?'

'That I'm to lie to everyone except you and Ma.'

'And me,' Shane butted in. 'You're not to lie to me neither.'

'Oh, yeah — and not to Aunty Lisa,' Tommy added.

'And the whole family,' Michael instructed. 'You never lie to anyone in the family. Understand?'

Tommy nodded solemnly. 'Tell us the story about the Mansions, Da. When the whole family was living together in the one place.'

'Fair enough. You want to hear the whole thing?'

'From the start.'

Shane snuggled into his pillow. 'Tell us it from the very first beginning, Da. From the bit that starts, "Once upon a time..."'

'Okay.' Michael grinned and settled himself on the

floor between the two beds. 'Okay, once upon a time...'

Shane smiled with contentment.

'Long, long ago,' Michael continued, 'years before you were born, when your ma and me and Aunty Lisa were very young, we all lived in a place called the Mansions. A block of flats. And everyone was in this one place, all our grannies and granddads and brothers and sisters, and all our pals. It was brilliant. It was like a big hotel specially built for us and all our mates.

'Everyone had a special talent, and we all knew the best person to go to for whatever we needed. Tony Brady was great at slipping into the wholesalers' and nicking cartons of cigarettes to give to our fathers and all our uncles. It was the only way they could get a smoke, you see? Most of them were on the dole, and in those days the dole really wasn't worth picking up, so little it was. A few bob, that's all. There would never have been enough food to go round if we lads hadn't gone out every day and robbed some from the shops.'

Michael chuckled. 'But no one in the wholesalers' ever suspected it was Tony Brady nicking the cigarettes, because he was so small and timid-looking in those days, and he had such an angelic face. Ugly oul' face he's got on him now, of course. But me and Tony were always great pals.'

'You've never smoked, have you, Da?'

'No, Tommy. There's three things I've never done: smoked cigarettes, drunk alcohol or taken drugs. And that's a fact. And listen — I'll batter the life out of both of you if I ever learn you've gone anywhere near drugs, do you hear me?'

'Tell us more about the Mansions,' Shane urged.

Michael sat for a long, thoughtful moment, remembering the poverty and deprivation of life in the Dublin slums. What he remembered most was the hunger. And what he had hated most was the condescending attitude of the police, and society in general, towards those who lived on the edge of the breadline, on the wrong side of the tracks.

'Come on, Da!'

'Ah, the Mansions was a great place, so it was,' Michael continued with a smile. 'All the flats — over a hundred flats, there was, built just like a military barracks. And the square was always teeming with people. Kids running round having fun. Women hanging out of the windows gossiping. Lads playing marbles or toss-penny. And what made it so great was the way everyone knew everyone else, and the way we all looked out for each other. It wasn't much to look at, the Mansions, but it was our kingdom, and the place we all called *home.*'

Michael frowned. 'And then the bailiffs came... There were loads of them, and they were huge. And you know what bailiffs are?'

'They're like the gardaí, only worse,' said Tommy.

'Much worse. So one day — this was after your ma and I had got married and not long after you were born, Shane — this one day I was coming home after working hard ... and I saw them. The bailiffs, attacking our homes. Loads of the big bastards. Beating down the doors of the flats with lump hammers. And officers of the gardaí standing by and backing them.'

'Did you fight with them?'

'Yeah, I fought with them, of course I did. Tony and the others, too. We all fought with them. There was loads of punching and head-bashing, and I did good work on about ten of them, but there were too many altogether. So your ma and me and Lisa locked ourselves into our flat and barricaded the place.

'"No, you're not taking our home from us, no matter what," we said. And they couldn't get in, no matter how hard they tried. They were rightly fucked off, I'm telling you. And in the days that followed, all we could hear around us was the screaming and wailing of our friends and neighbours as their houses were being torn down, demolished, because the Corporation wanted the land for some other use.

'And every time we peeped out the window, all we could see was our neighbours being driven out of the Mansions, never to return. And who was standing by, overseeing the whole operation? The gardaí.

'But they couldn't get *us* out. We were barricaded in and we weren't moving. They tried everything to get us out. But they didn't know me. I wouldn't budge. No matter if they brought the whole place down around our ears. And no matter what they said to me through the window ... well, I just kept on smiling at them.

'All kinds of people came to try and talk to me, all high-ups from the Corporation. They needed the land to start building some other property on it. But I wasn't going to be kicked out like a rat in an alley.

'"No way," I said. "Yous can go fuck yourselves, or, alternatively, yous can give me a decent new place to live in. Otherwise I'm not budging."

'By this time, of course, all our neighbours were gone, and our flat was the only one still standing. All the rest of the place had been reduced to rubble by the big machines they used. But we didn't care; we were making our stand as a matter of principle.'

'And then the Mayor came,' Tommy grinned.

'What? Oh, yeah...' Michael had embellished the part about the Mayor a bit, to make the story more interesting.

'Well, they were so pissed off that they couldn't get the better of me, the Lord Mayor of Dublin himself came out to see your da...'

Tommy and Shane giggled. This was their favourite bit.

'A long fleet of black, shining cars pulled up at the flat, and out steps the Lord Mayor of Dublin himself, wearing a big gold chain around his neck. He begged me to leave. He said he was sorry for the way our family had been treated. Very, very sorry. But if I moved out, we would be given a lovely new Corporation house to live in.

'I made him swear to that. I made him promise in front of the witnesses — I made him get down on his knees and promise — and he did. He got down on his knees and he said, "Yes, I promise."

'And so we got our nice new Corporation house to live in. The house that Aunty Lisa lives in now.'

Michael smiled. 'I won in the end, boys. I beat them all, the bailiffs and the Mayor and the law. I was loyal, and that's why I won.' He sat for a moment savouring his victory. 'You see, the thing is, they'll never beat you if you stick together and stay loyal. And that's what your ma and me and Aunty Lisa did.'

'Stick together and stay loyal,' Tommy repeated.

'Stick together and stay loyal,' Shane echoed.

Michael smiled. 'After all, boys, that's what all good friends and all good families do.'

*

Christine was still up when Michael went downstairs. She was sitting at the kitchen table, her head bent over the book she had bought that day in Eason's.

'What're you reading?'

'A book about Caravaggio. You know, the artist that painted the picture I put up in the bedroom — *The Taking of Christ*.'

Her voice was strange and she kept her head lowered,

as though she didn't want to look up and meet Michael's eyes.

'You okay?'

Christine kept her head down. 'Yes.'

Michael stood looking at her, concerned, because he had suddenly noticed her body was shaking as if she was crying. But before he could say another word, she looked up at him and spluttered with laughter.

He smiled, relieved to see she was okay. 'What's so funny?'

'Caravaggio — there was me thinking he was some kind of artistic saint, but according to this, he was a fecking *criminal*.'

*C*hapter *Seven*

Michael spent the following day locked away in the small corner room at the end of the hall, busily writing and contemplating his notes, finalising his plan.

He had been thinking about it for months, working out how it could be done, considering every obstacle, every mistake a man might easily make, and everything that could possibly go wrong with the operation.

He sat back in the leather armchair and tapped his teeth with his pen. Now he was certain that it *could* be done — even though the IRA had decided a year ago that it could not.

They had cased the place, all right, with a view to a heist; but even with the help of sophisticated weaponry, and a potential reward of gold and jewels worth over two million pounds, the IRA had shaken their heads and walked away, saying it couldn't be done.

Political tossers — what did they know?

*

A week later, the chosen gang were summoned to the house for a meeting. Minutes after they arrived, there was a buzz of anticipation and high spirits in the living-room. All of them knew a job was on. A big one.

It was Sunday afternoon, the summer weather very warm. The children were playing in the front garden, with Lisa joining in. Christine was busy in the kitchen preparing a tray of sandwiches. To any outsider watching the house, nothing untoward was going on — just Michael Lynch and a few of his friends getting together to drink beer and watch the football match on the telly.

Tony Brady was late arriving. He lifted up Breda and swung her around.

'I hear you're making your Holy Communion, honey-bunch. Like my Declan. Remember Declan? He wants to marry you, d'you know that?'

Breda screamed with laughter and ran to Christine.

Although Tony Brady and Stevie Brady had the same surname, they were not brothers, nor even related. Tony had a face like granite and was built like a stone door, but underneath his tough exterior, he was a tender-hearted and kind man.

Stevie Brady was the opposite. He was thirty-two and attractive, and he always dressed in blue denim from collar to ankle — jeans and jackets, and often a denim shirt as well. He looked cheery and confident, but underneath his sunny appearance he worried like a woman; he suspected everyone and everything, always fearing the worst.

Michael's brother, Billy, was in charge of the bottle opener. 'There you go,' he said merrily, giving a bottle of beer to Tom Rooney. Then he opened another bottle and grinned like a round-faced cupid as he handed it to Shay Kirby; his curly fair hair added to the illusion, making him look younger than his twenty-eight years.

Michael's drink, as always, was non-alcoholic. Today

it was fresh orange juice. He was standing by the window, watching Billy. There was something about his brother that was beginning to trouble him. Over the past few months, Billy had changed from the casual and easy-going person he had always been. These days Billy was either dour or hyper, one or the other, never a mid-way balance between the two. Today he was hyper and full of enthusiasm, like a cheerful puppy scampering around a group of lazy dogs.

'Here you go, Tony!' Billy held out a bottle of beer to the latecomer. 'Just give me a shout when you want another, yeah?'

'Yeah.' Tony nodded.

'The first one for the couch,' Billy laughed. 'The last one for the road. And as much as you like in between.'

Stevie Brady had sidled over to Michael by the window. He looked troubled and spoke low.

'Michael ... your new fella, Shay Kirby. It doesn't bother you that he used to be in the IRA?'

'Nah. He's been out a couple of years.'

'Bit dodgy, though, isn't it? Why are you bringing him in?'

Michael got tired of Stevie sometimes. 'He's the inside man, that's why I'm bringing him in.'

'The inside man?'

'On the new job I'm going to tell all of you about. Look, to allay your fears, Stevie, while I'm talking I'll make a crack about the Provos, and you watch how he reacts.'

Stevie shrugged. He didn't think Michael was taking the point seriously enough, but he let it pass.

But, as he stood drinking his beer, Stevie couldn't help worrying about it. He had always maintained that the IRA and other political rousers lived in a very different world from ordinary decent criminals. They had different rules, different end-games, a whole different mentality.

No, Stevie was not happy about the inclusion of Shay Kirby, not happy at all.

Christine stood by the door, calling up the stairs. 'Tommy, come on, we're going. Tommy, move it! We'll be late for the trailers. Breda, say goodbye to Daddy.'

Michael had sat down in his favourite armchair. Breda jumped into his arms and gave him a kiss.

'Ahh, chicken,' Michael smiled. 'You enjoy yourself, now.'

Christine picked up her handbag and looked at Michael. 'You have everything you need?'

'We're grand. Go on, will you.'

'Right. Good luck, so.'

Lisa popped her head round the door and waved to the room. 'Bye, lads.'

Billy Lynch couldn't help snickering to himself. He nudged Alec Duignan, beside him, and whispered in his ear, 'Two for the price of one, hah?'

Alec frowned sharply at him, warning Billy to shut up in case Michael heard. The strange and unconventional relationship between Michael and the two sisters was a forbidden subject for gossip, even amongst his friends.

Now the women and children had gone, Michael took charge. 'All right, lads. Everyone sitting down?'

The six men sat themselves around the room. On the long coffee table in the centre was an array of beer bottles, a jug of fresh orange juice and ice, and a tray of chicken and tuna-salad sandwiches.

'Right,' Michael said. 'Now, as you know, from Monday week I'm going to be a bit occupied in the Four Courts on a robbery charge. It should go okay, but you never know. So I thought maybe now was the time to do a job I've been thinking about for the last few months.'

Every man was attentive.

'One of those so-called impossible jobs. Worth about two million. Now this is one the IRA had their eyes on, but they thought it couldn't be done. Well, once I heard that,' Michael said with boastful good humour, 'I thought — we're going to have to show those dozy fuckers a thing or two about robbing, yeah?'

Amidst the general laughter, Stevie watched Shay Kirby, who was also chuckling merrily, and genuinely so... Maybe he had been worrying unnecessarily and it was all right.

'What's the job?' Tony asked.

'O'Donnell's Jewellery Factory,' Michael said smoothly. He was pleased to see the look of astonishment on all their faces, except for Shay Kirby's — he already knew.

The rest just stared at him.

Billy was the first to speak. 'Fuck me.'

'O'Donnell's Jewellery Factory?' Tony couldn't believe it. 'I knew you were fucking nuts.'

'Can't be done,' Stevie said simply. 'If the IRA cased it and walked away, then we shouldn't touch it.'

Michael didn't look surprised by their reaction. He shrugged. 'Okay. If you don't want a share of two million, that's okay with me. But I'm telling you, we can do it. I know we can. I'm sure of it.'

Tony said cautiously, 'Why are you so sure we can do it?'

'Because when it comes to robbery, the IRA are amateurs compared to us. We've been doing it all our lives. We're past masters. It's the only game we play, the only one we know, and we're the best. Isn't that true?'

No one felt able to deny it. They *were* the best.

Michael smiled coaxingly. 'Imagine this, lads. In a week or so, we could be standing somewhere looking at mounds of sparkling jewels and gleaming gold bars. And even after the fences have screwed us, we should each be at least fifty thousand quid richer.'

Alec was already game for it. 'Yes!'

Billy looked more enthusiastic now. Tony and Stevie looked at each other; then Tony looked questioningly at Michael. 'First things first. Tell us the details.'

Michael stood up, his face serious. 'Right, the details... O'Donnell's Jewellery Factory has a very secure high wall. We all know that. Twenty feet high, to be exact. Sensor alarms all along the top — touch it anywhere and you're fucked. All the doors are fully alarmed, all high-tech stuff in the security field, so they've no need for any night guard. But before we even get inside, the biggest hassle will be getting past the outside wall.'

'So how do we?' Stevie asked.

Michael went on as if there had been no interruption. 'And then there's the locals, in the block of flats next door, watching everything that goes on. Well, usually, but I think we can find a way around that.'

'How?' Billy asked.

Michael said impatiently, 'Little fella — shut up.'

Billy eyed the bottle in his hand. 'Just asking.'

'And then, even if we do get past the wall,' Michael continued, 'the alarm system for the main building is connected to a garda station not five hundred yards away. So there's no point in even trying to break in. That's what the IRA thought. But not me. I can see a way straight in.'

The room was silent. Everyone was staring at him, baffled.

'It just *seems* pointless and impossible,' Michael explained. 'But that's only to amateurs who think every big job must be done in a fancy way, with lots of clever manoeuvres and cross-contacting the wires of a closed-circuit system and all that high-tech crap.'

He smiled. 'Sure, a job must be meticulously planned, but it can still be done with the minimum of fuss and trouble. Like I've always said at the beginning of every job we've ever done — keep it simple.'

Tony was looking utterly flummoxed. 'So how've you worked it out?'

Michael shrugged. 'I've worked it out the same way any kid in that block of flats next door to O'Donnell's Factory would work it out, if he wanted to get in badly enough. A kid's way — simple.'

'Tell us the plan,' Stevie said impatiently.

Billy piped up. 'Is it a foolproof plan?'

Michael gave his brother an amused smile. 'How can it be a foolproof plan, Billy, when you're going to be in on it?'

Billy laughed along with the men. He was basically good-natured, and he knew Michael was only joking.

'So my plan is this,' Michael continued. 'We wouldn't even bother trying to break into the factory itself. But we *could* drop into O'Donnell's during the night. What you might call a *flying visit*.'

Michael laughed at their reaction. 'You know, it's going to be such a breeze. So simple...' His face was still twitching with mirth.

'But first, we've got to get in a little practice. So for the next few nights I want you all to come out with me to the Wicklow Mountains. I've found just the spot for us.'

Before anyone could say a word, Michael added a warning. 'I've only one proviso. The robbery has to be done next week or not at all.'

Stevie asked cautiously, 'Why's that?'

'Because next week is the start of the two-week summer-holiday break. O'Donnell's workforce will be reduced to a skeleton staff ... which, of course, is just perfect for us.'

Chapter Eight

A week later they were ready.

The Corporation block of flats next to O'Donnell's Jewellery Factory was of the old style, built in the 1950s, and only four storeys high — thirty-eight feet high in all. The windows of the flats were at the front and back, not in the side overlooking the factory.

And all the windows of the flats were now in darkness, everyone asleep.

Michael flipped his wrist and glanced at the luminous red figures on his digital watch. It was 3.45 in the morning.

'Okay, time to go,' he whispered.

Silently and swiftly, he led the men up the stairs of the flats to the tower of the block. On the roof of the flats, they prepared themselves and their equipment. All were dressed like mountaineers about to go abseiling.

Michael peered at the men in the darkness and asked, 'Everyone prepared?'

Everyone was prepared, but Michael sensed a deep current of fear and tension in the men, and he was right.

None of them were kids, and they were frightened that it couldn't be done so easily. All they had to assure them was Michael's word for it. He had even gone so far as to guarantee their safety. No one would get hurt. They had practised and done it safely numerous times in the mountains, so they could do it just as well here.

'Anyone want to back out?' Michael asked.

No man wanted to back out, but that didn't stop them from being frightened.

'Look,' Michael said confidently, 'it's going to be a breeze. We're all in this together, we have a job to do. So let's make it fun.'

He grinned at them in the darkness. 'And, like any good leader, I'll go first.'

No more words were spoken as the plan was put into operation. Michael took out a lethal-looking contraption — a mix between a crossbow and a harpoon gun. Attached to it was a grappling-hook and a thin, but very strong, cable.

He took a strong stance and aimed at the roof of O'Donnell's Factory. He shot the grappling-hook over, almost twenty feet above the sensor alarm; it hit the flat roof.

Everyone breathed a sigh of relief.

'Now pull slowly,' Michael whispered.

Tony and Stevie pulled the cable and watched the grappling-hook moving slowly until it caught on the parapet of the roof, well lodged underneath it.

Tony gave it a strong tug, and nodded. 'It's well caught underneath. It won't budge.'

'Any slack on the cable?' Michael asked.

'No slack, dead tight,' Stevie said. He checked the iron hand-ring on the cable. 'All set.'

Michael took a deep breath and stood on the edge of the roof of the flats. He looked over his shoulder at the men and grinned. 'After this, we'll all be able to join the Gladiators. You know — those guys on TV. That's where I got the idea from.'

And then he was flying through the air, his gloved hands gripping the iron hand-ring tight as it slid down the cable towards O'Donnell's roof at a faster speed than Michael had anticipated. The drop was lower than the one in the mountains. The grooved rubber soles of his mountain boots were two inches thick, cushioning the impact as his feet hit the wall just below the parapet. For a second or two he just hung there; then he swung up a leg and pulled himself over the parapet and onto the roof.

He grinned and gave the thumbs-up to the men on the roof of the flats. The hook and cable had held strongly, and the flight through the air had been just as he had said it would be — a breeze.

Tony Brady was the next man to follow. As soon as his boots hit the wall, Michael was waiting to give him a hand up onto the roof. Then they both helped up Stevie, Billy, Tom Rooney and Shay Kirby.

Only Alec Duignan remained on the roof of the flats. He would not be making the slide. The cable was wrapped securely around a broad brick chimney-outlet on the top of the flats. Alec unwrapped it and carried it over to the edge of the roof, letting Michael slowly pull in the slack on the cable until it was tight between their hands, twenty feet above the sensor alarm.

Alec took a deep breath. Everything now depended upon the strength of his throw and Michael's pull at the same time.

'Now!' Michael called.

Alec flung, and Michael pulled fast enough for the cable not to drop anywhere near the sensor alarm, but clear the wall about ten feet above it.

Again everyone let out a breath of relief. They were in, and so was the cable. Nothing left hanging for anyone on the street outside to see.

Billy was laughing quietly. 'That was great fun,' he said, now the danger was over. 'Flying through the air like that, I felt like a kid again.'

'Stop laughing and start moving,' Michael ordered.

The cable was rolled into a thick loop, the grappling-hook dislodged, and then they made their descent into the yard below by the steps of the fire escape on the outside wall of the factory.

Down in the yard, Michael removed the haversack from his back, taking out a roll of red canvas. Stevie and Tony removed their backpacks and took out the rods. Michael unrolled the canvas tent. From his bag, Tom Rooney unclipped the three wooden sections of the main pole and fitted them together. There would be four poles in all.

Unrolled and erected, it was a larger tent than the men had expected. 'Plenty of room for us all,' Michael grinned.

Inside the tent, sitting down on a thin sheet of plastic, the men all looked at Michael for more details and their next instructions.

'Well, the next part is very simple,' Michael told them. 'All we do now is camp out here in the yard, and wait until someone arrives to let us into the factory in the morning.'

*

That someone was Mr Fintan Doorley, the General Manager.

Michael had been watching Fintan Doorley on and off for months, and what he had observed on every occasion was that Mr Doorley was a man who obviously liked and needed a strict routine. A very precise man, who always arrived at the factory at five minutes to eight every morning.

This morning was no exception.

Fintan Doorley arrived precisely on time at five minutes to eight, bypassing the main gate, as always, and stopping at the smaller door a few yards beyond it. He keyed in the security code to open the door and entered. The door closed automatically behind him.

As he turned the corner of the yard, the unexpected sight of a bright red tent parked in the middle of it made him stop in shock.

Michael and Shay Kirby, both armed, stepped out to greet him. Tony and Stevie followed.

'Ah, we've sent you into shock, Mr Doorley,' Michael said sympathetically. 'We're sorry for that. All we want is your keys to the factory.'

Mr Doorley was indeed in shock at what he saw: hooded men, *hoodlums,* armed with guns. But *how* had they got in? O'Donnell's security was impregnable.

'I know your old ticker isn't the best, so I hope the shock of all this hasn't sent your pacemaker out of control.'

'My *what*?'

Michael's tone was sympathetic. 'It must be hard for you, the worry of a bad heart. Do the top bosses here know that you have it, by the way — the pacemaker? Do they know that you're such a terrible liability?'

Fintan Doorley was losing his breath. 'How did you — there's *nothing wrong* with my heart. And if you hoodlums think you can intimidate —'

'Nothing wrong with your heart?' Michael said. 'Oh, well now, let's see if that's true...'

He reached inside his jacket and took out a large magnet. Shay Kirby grabbed Doorley and pinned his arms back.

Michael held the magnet high in the air with his left hand, while ripping open Doorley's jacket and shirt with his right hand. 'No pacemaker, no problems caused by the magnet — eh, Mr Doorley?'

Fintan Doorley stared at the magnet moving closer to his chest, and screamed. 'Stop, stop! The keys...'

Shay Kirby let go.

Doorley produced the keys.

*

Inside the factory, having turned off all the high-tech alarms, Fintan Doorley was looking pale and ill. Now he understood how the captain of the *Titanic* must have felt when he realised his unsinkable ship was actually sinking.

'Now the strongroom,' Michael said.

Escorted by the two hooded men, Fintan Doorley led the way to the strongroom; but once there, he hesitated nervously. Michael sighed, and took out the magnet again...

Doorley lifted his hand and quickly rolled and clicked the combination lock back and forth, then stopped and stepped back, closing his eyes and lowering his head as if exhausted.

Michael pulled on the handle of the heavy metal door, and it opened. Within the strongroom he saw another safe.

'What's in there?'

'Diamonds.'

'Open it.'

Fintan Doorley sighed heavily as he walked into the strongroom and opened the safe.

'Thank you, Mr Doorley,' Michael said pleasantly. 'You see, it's always the way: if people don't harm us, we never harm them. Now, why don't the three of us go along to your office?'

*

Inside Doorley's office, after the poor man had been bound and gagged, Michael returned to the strongroom while Shay Kirby sat down at Doorley's desk and turned on a monitor. On screen appeared a view of the pavement and road outside the small door.

Shay knew the routine well. He was the 'inside man' because he had been working at O'Donnell's for over six months now. But Fintan Doorley, the General Manager, could not have recognised him in his balaclava; nor could he have recognised Shay's voice, because Shay had not spoken a word.

Now Shay did what Mr Doorley normally did every morning — monitored the arrival of the staff.

Normally the factory staff at O'Donnell's numbered more than a hundred, but due to the annual two-week break for the summer holiday, that number had been reduced to twenty-five. Shay himself was supposed to be on his holiday break from O'Donnell's.

The factory staff began to arrive at the small door. The first, two women, buzzed the intercom and looked up at the camera.

Shay pressed a button to let them in.

Inside the yard, the two women turned the corner and stopped dead — as shocked as Mr Doorley to be greeted by a red tent and three hooded and armed men, Tony and Billy and Tom Rooney, who ushered them into the tent to be tied up and gagged.

And so it went on:

Staff members arriving at the small door, buzzing the intercom and looking up at the camera.

Shay at the monitor, pressing the button — and, just like Mr Doorley, he let in no more than two at a time.

Staff turning the corner of the yard, being grabbed by Billy, Tom and Tony and ushered into the tent to be bound and gagged alongside their colleagues.

When everyone was in, Shay pressed a button and opened the main gate to let Alec drive a Hiace van in, then pressed another button to close the gate behind him.

Alec drove the van to the corner of the yard and jumped out, running round to open the back doors and leap inside; seconds later, aided by Billy, he lifted down Michael's Kawasaki motorbike, which had been fitted with false number-plates, and parked it by the wall.

Now that Alec and the van were safely inside, the rest of the men ran into the main building and joined Michael in the strongroom, where he had already filled a number of coal-sacks with gems and gold bars.

'Get to work, and fast,' he commanded. 'We've only got twenty-five minutes to load up and roll out before the office staff arrive at nine.'

Fifteen minutes later, audaciously led out by Michael on his motorbike, the Hiace van — loaded with jewels and gold and men — drove out of O'Donnell's main gate, leaving the factory staff bound and gagged in the tent, and Fintan Doorley bound and gagged in his office.

*

The report of the robbery reached the gardaí twenty minutes after the Hiace van had been driven out of the yard.

Five minutes after that, Detective Sergeant Noel Quigley arrived on the scene, surrounded by squad cars and uniformed police.

But Quigley knew they were already far too late. 'The van could have gone in any direction,' he said, 'once it got out on the streets.'

Every member of staff was questioned, but apart from the hoods and the guns, none could tell them anything about the men.

'Except...' one woman piped up, 'they all had Dublin accents. But then,' she shrugged, 'doesn't everyone in Dublin?'

Every resident of the adjoining block of flats was questioned, but all had heard no evil and seen no evil, which Quigley thought was 'bloody suspicious'.

He looked at Barry Kavanagh. 'Someone's nobbled them, either with money or with threats. I'm sure of it.'

Chapter Nine

The television and newspapers were in a frenzy. All the media telephone lines were buzzing. Headlines toppled over one another to report the robbery of gold and gems worth over two million pounds from O'Donnell's Jewellery Factory: *The biggest and most brazen robbery in Irish history.*

*

The Hiace van was on fire. It had been dumped on a remote road on the northern outskirts of Dublin, covered in petrol and set alight.

The gardaí were jubilant at finding the Hiace so soon. They had no doubt that it was the van used in the robbery. They never once suspected that it might be a duplicate, which had been hidden for a week in the garage of an accomplice, then driven out early in the morning and set alight at exactly nine o'clock, even before the alarm at O'Donnell's was raised.

'We have the van,' Noel Quigley informed Commissioner Daly.

'Are you sure it's the one used in the robbery?'

Noel Quigley nodded. 'I'm positive, sir. We even

found a couple of scorched gold watches on the floor of the burnt-out van.'

*

The Hiace used in the robbery had been reversed into a huge empty warehouse on the south side of Dublin, less than thirty minutes after it had left O'Donnell's.

'You see, it's all in the planning,' Michael had said. 'Every aspect of a job must be carefully planned, right down to the smallest detail. *Failing to plan is planning to fail* — that's my motto in everything. That and my old mantra, *Keep it simple.*'

It had been a long night without rest, followed by a long day, in which Michael and Tony had done all the sorting and counting while the others went home to get some sleep.

But now another night had fallen, and the men stood in the warehouse staring at the mounds of jewels and gold bars which were laid out on two snooker tables, all divided into equal shares for every man.

Magical in pools of light, the mounds of gold and jewels gleamed, and the men just stood and stared at them, unable to move as they drank in the beauty of the sight before their eyes.

Stevie finally turned thoughtfully to young Alec. 'What are you — twenty? Eight or ten years younger than me and Billy, right? Big difference. And then Tony and Michael are another ten years older than that, just on forty. But when they were kids, they had fuck all. Isn't that right, Michael, when you were kids?'

'We had each other.' Michael smiled. 'Okay, lads, it's all yours. One pile each. Take your pick, they're all equal.'

Stevie continued to chat to Alec as they bagged their

loot. 'Now I'm a bit younger than them, so I got some stuff as a kid, but it was never the right stuff.'

Alec looked at Stevie, more confused than ever. 'What're you gobshiting about?'

'Billy knows what I'm talking about, don't you, Billy?'

'No.'

Stevie continued bagging his loot, but his mind was thinking. 'Ah, fuck,' he said to Alec, 'what was the big thing when you were ... about eight, say?'

'What?'

'You know, the big toy that every kid wanted. What was it?'

'Ah — *Star Wars*, I suppose. Is that what you mean?'

'Exactly!' Stevie nodded. 'Now I bet you got the proper *Star Wars* stuff. The *real* toys. What were they called...?'

'The Luke Skywalker doll, Darth Vader... Sure, yeah.'

'And it was the proper thing? You know, the *official* stuff?'

'Yeah — so?' Alec still couldn't understand what Stevie was going on about.

'Well, I never got that,' Stevie said, 'never got the real thing. Not like you getting Darth Vader.'

Alec went on the defensive. 'But, sure, me da probably robbed it.'

'Doesn't matter,' Stevie insisted. 'My da couldn't even rob the proper thing. Like, now, Scalextric — that was the dream when I was a kid.'

Billy laughed. 'Yeah, that's right — and Subbuteo.'

'Fuck Subbuteo,' Stevie said. 'Scalextric is what we're talking about. It was the *name*, you see. The ad on the TV. That's what we kids all wanted, the same as the ad on the TV. So what did I get? Some other racing-car thing, some crap cheap imitation that was supposed to be like it. But it was *nothing* like it.'

Stevie was getting upset as he remembered. 'And Meccano. Did you ever hear of that? I never got the real Meccano set. I got some other ... crap!'

Alec looked at him sadly. 'That's a tragedy, Stevie.'

'It is, yeah, that's what I'm saying.' Stevie nodded, bagging a handful of top-carat diamonds. 'But Tony and Michael there — they never got anything except suckie sweets. Imagine! Me and Billy got stuff, all right, but it was some crap cheap version of the thing I really wanted.'

Stevie studied a diamond. 'Fellas your age always got the proper toy, though, and now my own kids expect every fuckin' thing that's going.'

Alec grinned, understanding at last. 'And now you're going to use all your dosh to make sure your kids get it, aren't you?'

'In my hole!' Stevie shook his head impatiently. 'I'm going to make up for the stuff *I* missed out on. I'm going to buy myself a brand-new Scalextric. I'm going to enjoy myself. Hey, Michael!'

'Yeah.'

Stevie was smiling like a boy. 'I have to say it, man. Fair dues to you.'

Michael nodded. 'And you, Stevie.'

'Yeah, fair dues to you, Michael,' Tom Rooney called out. 'You done us proud!'

All the gang agreed, whooping and cheering and rattling their jewellery.

Michael stood watching them, a quiet smile on his face, looking very contented with life.

I've made asses of the gardaí again, he was thinking. *Really horsed the pricks up this time — biggest robbery ever done in Ireland, wha'?*

He had to stop smiling and laugh.

Chapter ten

But a week later, in court, the gardaí had everything on their side. They had the charge, the prosecution, the right and might of the law, and even the judge. Especially the judge, ever since Judge O'Hare had heard a rumour that Michael Lynch was responsible for another robbery — O'Donnell's.

All Michael had to bring into court was his guilt, a crooked solicitor, and an ethically ambivalent barrister who liked huge cash backhanders for every appearance.

Fergus Harrison rose to his feet. 'Your Honour, may I make an application to adjourn proceedings until Wednesday —'

'Application denied.'

The speed of the interruption shocked even Harrison.

'But, your Honour —'

'Mr Harrison,' said Judge O'Hare, 'the prosecution is ready, the jury is ready, and *I* am ready. Your client cannot avoid the process of the law indefinitely.' He looked in the direction of the prosecution. 'Mr McHale, are you ready to begin?'

Fergus Harrison sat down and shot a glance at Michael. Now they knew *exactly* what to expect from this judge — trouble.

Michael glanced quickly around the room, and saw Detective Sergeant Noel Quigley looking at him with a big smirk on his face — a smirk that said, *You're fucked, Lynch.*

McHale was on his feet, addressing the jury. 'Almost two years ago, on 19 February 1990, the defendant, Michael Lynch, together with an unknown associate, entered the offices of Superex, a video-game company. They were armed and dangerous. They threatened the life of a member of staff, and they stole over thirty-two thousand pounds in cash...'

The rigmarole went on and on...

Michael sat back with his head bowed and a hand over his face, uninterested. His mind was miles away, untouched by the accusations and potential peril of the proceedings; he was protecting himself from anxiety in the way he always did, by dreaming up great plans for the future.

He was so lost in his thoughts, he didn't even realise that Noel Quigley had taken the stand, until Harrison nudged him to confer.

'This is a dangerous one,' Harrison whispered. 'His attitude is more personal than professional.'

'... And based upon the evidence you had gathered,' McHale said to Quigley, 'you concluded that it was a Michael Lynch operation.'

'Absolutely,' Quigley replied. 'You see, the accused is a very clever man —'

'Objection, your Honour,' Harrison called. 'This is opinion, not evidence.'

'Overruled.'

Harrison could take no more. O'Hare had overruled every single objection he had made so far, and, in some instances, very unfairly.

'Your Honour, if I may respectfully —'

'As an experienced police officer, Detective Sergeant Quigley is entitled to draw conclusions from his investigations,' O'Hare snapped. 'And the *jury* may decide if they are fair and reasonable. That is up to them.' He turned to the witness. 'Please continue, Detective Sergeant Quigley. You were about to explain to us exactly what a Michael Lynch operation is.'

'Yes, the accused —'

'*And will the accused sit up and let us see his face, please!*' O'Hare snapped out his interruption like the snarl of a pit bull.

Michael slowly removed his hands from his face and looked directly at the judge.

At that moment Fergus Harrison turned to look at his client and felt a sudden shock. He had always perceived Michael Lynch to be an amiable scoundrel, a joker who often trod on very dangerous ground. But in that one moment, he had seen a look of pure hatred on Lynch's face as he stared up at the judge.

But the judge didn't seem to have registered the danger of that look. He ordered Noel Quigley to continue.

'The accused,' said Quigley, 'is a genuinely clever man. Exceptionally so. But the odd thing is that he can't help letting people *know* how clever he is. He's just a big show-off who thinks he can get away with any crime he commits.'

As Harrison objected to this further allowance of mere opinion, Noel Quigley looked straight at Michael, and there was that smirk of his again...

Michael looked away, pretending boredom, but thinking, *It's you that's going to be fucked, Quigley, you and that judge along with you.*

*

At the close of the first week of the trial, walking out of the court, Fergus Harrison was extremely agitated. 'I don't often lose a case, Lynch, but I think I might lose this one.'

'Why?'

'Why? Isn't it obvious? The judge is blatantly endeavouring to turn the jury against us at every opportunity.'

'So what can we do about that?'

'I don't know *what* we can do. We need to pull some kind of rabbit out of a hat, but I'm no magician.' Harrison paused and pushed out his bottom lip. 'I know we should be optimistic to the end ... but I fear we *could* be looking at a stretch of ten to twelve years.'

'No.' Michael shook his head determinedly. 'Nobody's going to lock me away behind bars — no way. Not the gardaí, not Noel Quigley, and not even that bastard judge is going to do that.' Furious, he prodded his finger into Harrison's chest. 'And if those fucking pigs *are* winning the case — then what the hell am I paying *you* for?'

'Mr Lynch!'

But Michael didn't stop walking, and he didn't look back. He knew it was all down to him now. The trial was due to finish on Thursday, so he had only six days to try and find a rabbit in a hat.

*

Michael only used pubs as places to meet friends. He joined Shay Kirby at the bar.

'What'll it be?' Michael nodded at Shay's glass.

'No, I'm grand.' Shay looked at him questioningly. 'What's the problem?'

'This fucking judge is getting on my nerves,' Michael said. 'He's prejudiced, you know.'

Shay narrowed his eyes. 'Yeah?'

'Yeah.'

Michael took a sheet of paper from his pocket and passed it under Shay's palm. 'That's his daughter's car. The trial will be over by Thursday; does that give you enough time?'

Shay sipped his drink, and nodded. 'Consider it done.'

*

The gold bars stolen from O'Donnell's Jewellery Factory were now loaded in the boot of Tom Rooney's car, in readiness for transportation over to the fence in England.

Michael had drawn up the plan for their conveyance, but still Tom Rooney embarked on explaining at unnecessary length how the gold bars would be hidden, as if the plan was his own concept.

'It's brilliant, Michael. You see, the depth of the door is just right.' He opened the car door. 'Now, you see, once these panels are removed, the bars sit in there nice and snug. If you have enough of them, they don't rattle around, and you don't even notice the extra weight when you're opening and closing the door.'

'Okay,' Michael sighed patiently, 'I get it, Tom.'

'Now, this couple that I've lined up to take the gold over, they're complete innocents. That's the beauty of it — no extra splits. They're just old friends of me da's, going to England on their holidays, a couple in their sixties — Mr and Mrs Harmless, I've always called them. I know them well. They never drive at more than twenty-five miles an hour.'

'Yeah, fine, Tom, it all sounds fine.' Michael knew that Tom would talk for hours if he was let. He cuffed Tom on the shoulder and abruptly turned to leave. 'I'll see you when you get back, so. G'night.'

'Night, Michael. See ya in about two weeks from now, hah?'

*

On Wednesday night, Judge O'Hare was in fine form. He lived alone in a five-bedroomed house on the coast road to Bray, and tonight his twenty-six-year-old daughter, Nuala, had driven all the way out from her own small house in Dublin to have dinner with him and to introduce him to her new boyfriend.

The judge was sad when the time came for his daughter to leave. He opened the front door, and saw it was raining.

'You'd better run to the car if you don't want to get soaked,' he advised. But Nuala hesitated, always reluctant to say farewell to him. She was not happy about her father living alone, but she also needed to live a life of her own. And that life was now in the heart of Dublin.

'Give me the car keys, love,' her boyfriend said. 'I'll drive us back.' Then, to the judge, 'Thanks again, sir, for a very stimulating evening.'

He took the car keys and dashed into the rain.

'I hope we didn't outstay our welcome, Dad.'

'Not at all. Mind you, this new man of yours — he does like the sound of his own voice, doesn't he?'

'You're one to talk,' Nuala laughed. 'You're just annoyed that there's someone in this world who dares to argue back.'

The boyfriend was almost at the car. A second before he reached it, Shay Kirby hit the button on the remote-control device.

The blast of the explosion rocked through the air, sending the boyfriend flying flat onto his back.

For a moment, the judge and his daughter stood staring in horrified shock: the car was engulfed in flames.

Then Nuala screamed hysterically and tried to run

forward. Her father grabbed her and held her back —
releasing her only when he saw her boyfriend get to his
feet, stumbling back towards them in a daze.

Judge O'Hare's face was stark white, his eyes staring
at the burning car. He didn't know who had done this,
but he knew for certain *why* it had been done — to convey
a personal message to him from Michael Lynch.

*

The silence in the courtroom was deadly tense.

Detective Sergeant Noel Quigley was standing at the
back of the room, tight with rage.

Michael was gazing calmly at Judge O'Hare, who had
completely changed his tone and tune, and was now
making his final address to the jury.

'... And, in summation, whatever the jury's feelings
may be as to the most just conclusion to draw, I must
remind you that you are compelled *by law* to abide by the
strict requirements of evidence. And if the available
evidence is not sufficient for a conviction, then ... you
must not convict.'

*

'Here he comes!'

Michael emerged from the Four Courts to meet a
scrum of photographers and a barrage of questions from
journalists.

'You've been found not guilty, Michael, so can we see
your face now?'

'Mr Lynch, have you any comment to make on
rumours of intimidation?'

'Give us a wave, Michael.'

'Mr Lynch, 98FM. Can you reassure the people of Dublin that you are no threat to their safety?'

'What do you think of the gardaí now, Michael?'

From behind his balaclava, Michael grinned. He spotted Detective Sergeant Noel Quigley standing a few yards away; he brazenly raised his hand and gave him the thumbs-up.

Quigley turned away in disgust.

Christine and Lisa drove up to the front steps of the Four Courts building. Michael ran down to the car and waved to the photographers as if they were his pals. And, in a way, they were — he was a criminal anti-hero who always made headline news for them. Any article on Michael Lynch went straight onto the front page with a condemnatory headline, and sold out within hours.

More cameras flashed.

'How can you afford such an expensive legal team, Mr Lynch?'

'Are you still on the dole, Michael?'

Michael turned round, offended. 'Of course I'm still on the dole,' he shouted back. 'How else am I supposed to live and feed my family?'

'Take off the hood just a sec, would you? One smile?'

'Bye, lads!'

Michael slammed the car door behind him and nodded to Christine to get going.

A collective groan went up from the reporters as the car sped away.

*

On Monday evening, Detective Sergeant Noel Quigley arrived home earlier than usual.

He lived only a ten-minute drive from the Central Detective Unit in Harcourt Street, but, his work being what it was, he could never tie himself or his wife to a set time to dine. But tonight he had arrived home in time to eat with the family.

His wife was not that pleased. She hadn't been expecting him, so she had cooked only for the children. She brought two plates of burgers, chips and peas to the table and set them before the twins.

She looked apologetically at her husband. 'Shall I open a tin of soup for you? To keep you going until I cook something?'

'No, I'll wait.'

Noel felt annoyed at having to wait and take second place to the children. It was an irrational annoyance, because he loved his children and he loved the devoted way his wife looked after them; but tonight he regarded the wait for his dinner as an undermining of his individual power — the same individual power that all husbands and fathers should feel within their homes. After all, he was the breadwinner, the one who had to go out and slog for a living to bring home the money to keep the family going.

He sat at the table and tried to involve himself with the twins, pretending to be interested in their trivial chatter about friends at school, but really he was too fed up tonight to listen.

When his wife returned to the table, he stood up. 'I think I'll have a short nap before I eat.'

His wife looked at him in surprise, but she didn't dare question him because of the moody expression on his face. So she just nodded. 'All right. I'll call you when it's ready.'

Noel went up to his bedroom and pulled off his tie. He had no intention of taking a nap, but he needed to be alone.

He opened the locker on his side of the bed and took out a packet of cigarettes. He was trying to give up, to save money, but tonight he felt like indulging himself with a smoke.

He was smouldering with resentment. He had been cheated of his prize. With Lynch convicted and locked up, he could have moved on to the next job, and the next step towards promotion.

Now he was left with nothing to show for all his hard work, except the same old worries about mortgage payments, endless bills, children to be dressed. The endless scramble to make ends meet and clock up the overtime pay — but there were only seven days in a week.

Only promotion would get him the extra money he needed. And he would get that promotion somehow. Even with Commissioner Daly and Michael Lynch standing in his way, he would get it.

Chapter Eleven

Mr and Mrs Harmless had always loved the Cotswolds, although they hadn't been back there for a holiday in five years, favouring instead the reliable sunshine of Palma or Tenerife. But now they were sick of all that; sitting in the sun was one thing, but you got weary of it after a while, and there was nothing to stimulate the eyes or the mind. Nothing but sand and sea, and the hotel full of English lager-louts kicking up a stink every night.

Ah, but the Cotswolds were full of high and wide hills, and lovely English gardens filled with flowers of all colours. And the people were not only older, but so much more refined and *cultured* than the lager-louts.

And this trip was going to be full of culture, they had decided. A visit to Beverton Castle, then a trip down to Slad Valley, where Laurie Lee had written his book *Cider with Rosie*. Mr Harmless loved that book.

And after Slad Valley, a quick jaunt up the road to the lovely village of Bisley, where the romantic novelist Jilly Cooper lived. Mrs Harmless was determined to get her autograph — a souvenir to show off to all her neighbours and friends.

Ah yes, they had their holiday all planned, and it was

going to be just grand. And Tom Rooney, bless him, had given their car a free service for them — a complete overhaul of the engine, new spark-plugs and everything, and no charge at all for it.

'But didn't I always tell yeh that Tom Rooney was a decent fella,' Mr Harmless said repeatedly.

'Oh, very decent,' his wife unceasingly agreed.

And so they set off on their holiday, completely un-aware that the driver's door of their car was packed with half a million pounds' worth of stolen gold bars.

They had travelled over from Dublin to Holyhead on the car-ferry early that morning, and now they were waiting to drive through Customs.

Mr Harmless sat behind the wheel, staring straight ahead. He nodded his head towards the Customs men. 'It's drugs they'll be looking for. Lousy drugs.'

Mrs Harmless narrowed her eyes, her mouth turned down. 'That couple in front of us ... they look like druggies. I bet they are.'

The couple in front were driving a Citroën 2CV. He looked like a bearded radical, and she was obviously some kind of New-Age hippy. And, true to type, they were signalled to drive the Citroën in for inspection, while the old couple were waved on their way.

'Here we go!' Mr Harmless became gravely serious as he gunned up the engine to drive on. 'This is where we hit the road all the way to the Cotswolds.'

A Customs man smiled patiently and touched his hat to the old couple as their car chugged through at a speed of no more than ten miles an hour.

*

Mr Harmless had never liked the idea of driving on

motorways; the speed was just too fast altogether, too
dangerous. So he decided not to go on the speedier route
of the M5 motorway, but chose the slower and more
scenic route on the A5 to Shrewsbury, a journey that
would take them four hours if they drove at a speed of
thirty miles an hour.

'Sure, we've loads of time,' he said. 'It's only one o'clock,
and we don't have to check in at the hotel until eight.'

'Loads of time,' his wife agreed. 'And we can stop on
the way. I've got a pile of sandwiches packed for us here
in me bag. And two bottles of stout.'

'Ah, grand.'

*

Tom Rooney's flight landed two hours later at Birmingham
Airport. There he hired a rental car in a false name, using
a forged driving licence.

He drove out of the airport onto the M42, then sped
towards the M5 motorway, careful not to do a mile more
than the speed limit of seventy. He didn't want to risk
catching the attention of the motorway police.

The old couple had booked into a hotel in Great
Malvern, a four-to-five-hour drive from Holyhead, but
less than two hours' drive from Birmingham. Tom Rooney's
plan was to reach Great Malvern before they did.

Tom was familiar with the route. He had flown over to
England and driven down to Great Malvern three days
ago, to case the place, then flown back. All done in a day.

Tom sighed: with gold bars worth that kind of money,
and the risk taken to get them, Michael Lynch would
neither accept nor excuse mistakes.

On the drive down to Great Malvern, Tom went over
the plan again in his head...

The couple had booked into the Cotford Hotel on Graham Street, a big stone-house place built in the last century, with gardens full of flowers. So he had booked into the Great Malvern Hotel — also on Graham Street, but about fifty yards further up. He had given a false name, of course.

By the time he reached the Great Malvern Hotel, two hours later, Tom was feeling in fine form. He checked in at the desk, then went straight to his room and locked the door before taking out his mobile and calling the fence in Manchester.

'Yeah, sure thing,' he confirmed. 'Everything's going like clockwork. I'll have the car to you by two in the morning, half past two at the latest.'

*

The hotel had a brasserie and a bar. Tom decided to have an early dinner in the brasserie and follow it up with a few drinks afterwards in the bar.

He didn't like eating alone, but he worked manfully at his steak while relishing the plan. He smiled to himself as he chewed — it was going to be so fucking easy! Like taking sweeties from a baby!

He could see it all happening before his eyes. The old couple arriving at the Cotford Hotel down the road...

'Ah, lovely place,' she would say.

'Ah, grand,' he would agree.

Then up to their room to unpack their luggage, before lumbering back downstairs to have dinner; then an early night after all their travelling.

'Long oul' day,' he would say.

'Ah, yes,' she would agree tiredly.

Tom Rooney smiled; he knew them well... And once

they were back in their room and safely stretched out in bed, he would wander into the hotel's car park, take out his duplicate set of keys, and drive the car and the gold up to Manchester, where the fence and his mate would be waiting — ready to dismantle the door, remove the gold bars, then replace the panels and the door — and all in good time for Tom to do the two-hour drive back to the Cotford Hotel's car park before breakfast.

The couple would get up in the morning and set off in their car, sightseeing, and not suspect a thing.

Tom looked at his watch: 6.05. They should have arrived at their hotel by now.

*

'Ah, no!'

Mrs Harmless felt an unpleasant twitch of annoyance. They had been driving for miles along a nice country road, all leafy and green, and now her husband said it was the wrong one.

'But it *can't* be the wrong road.'

'Well, it *is* — that sign back there said this was the B4224, but we should be on the A449, so we *are* on the wrong road.'

'Stop shouting!'

'I'm *not* shouting — I'm dying for a leak, that's what I am. Me bladder is near to bursting.'

'Your bladder is *always* near to bursting.'

'Oh, wait now, here's another road sign... No, no, we're all right; if we carry on a couple of miles down this road, then we can turn right at the roundabout and head straight for Malvern.'

'Ah, that's good.' Mrs Harmless brightened. 'Sure, maybe it's all for the best, anyway. This way we can get a better look at the River Severn.'

Mr Harmless glanced at the waters of the Severn running just below the green bank at the side of the road, and felt his bladder churning.

'It's no good,' he said. 'I can't stand it a minute longer. I'll have to take a leak.' He stopped the car. 'I'll go over by that tree there.'

He opened the driver's door without checking behind. A Land Rover flew by without stopping — crashing past and taking the door off its hinges.

'*Jayyy-sus!*' Mr Harmless almost had a heart attack. The force of the bang had been as loud as a bomb.

Mrs Harmless was gulping frantically for breath. 'And th-they never even s-stopped, either!'

'Would you look at that!'

Horrified, they stared at the door of the car, on the opposite side of the road, further up, lying about a foot down the grassy bank.

'What're we going to do?' Mrs Harmless cried fretfully. 'We can't drive the car with no door on. Can we ring up one of the rescue places? The RAC?'

'How can we? There's no public telephone to ring anyone.' Mr Harmless looked around him. 'We're stuck out in the middle of nowhere. And anyway, I'm not a member of the RAC or any other English association, you *know* that.'

'So what're we going to do?'

Mr Harmless sat thinking about it for a minute, then shrugged his shoulders resignedly. 'I'll just have to try and fix the door back on meself. Come and give us a hand to lift it.'

They got out of the car and went over to the door lying on the side of the road, by the river's green sloping bank.

After a few minutes of heaving and pulling, they

straightened up and stared at each other in complete bewilderment. They couldn't lift the door. Not an inch could they lift it.

'I don't understand it.' Mr Harmless was feeling hot under the collar. He put a hand to the back of his neck. 'It's a ton weight. You wouldn't think a car door would be that heavy, would you?'

He didn't say any more.

Mrs Harmless didn't say anything either.

They just stood there like two befuddled fools, wondering what to do.

*

Four hours later, at 11.15 — earlier than the midnight time he had planned — Tom Rooney left his hotel and sauntered down the road towards the Cotford Hotel. The old couple would be tucked up peacefully in their beds by now, and their car parked waiting for him.

As he entered the car park he smiled. Ah, there it was: even in the dark he could see it from yards off — his little gold-mine.

In case anyone saw him, he approached the car with a casual confidence, as if he owned it, jangling the keys out of his pocket and walking round to the driver's side — jerking back with shock: the door was gone!

Tom just couldn't accept or understand it. The fucking driver's door was *gone* from the car!

And the gold bars with it!

Nervous ... terrified ... then consumed with rage, Tom turned and ran into the hotel, banging on the desk, demanding to be given the room number of the couple. It was an emergency, he was a close relative, no time could be lost.

*

'What...? Who...?'

Mr Harmless hadn't thought to lock the door of the room. He sat up, switched on the light, and stared in puzzlement at Tom Rooney.

Mrs Harmless sat up in her own twin bed also, blinking as if seeing a ghost.

'Tom — what're *you* doing here?'

Tom Rooney's heart was pounding and he contracted his body, forcing himself to stay calm and not give the plan away. 'I — I'm over for the big race at Cheltenham tomorrow. A sudden decision...'

Mrs Harmless looked disapproving, her mouth turned down. 'Horses — I've never agreed with gambling.'

Her husband was staring innocently at Tom. 'And are you staying at this hotel?'

'No, no ... I just dropped in to say hello to yous...' Tom could restrain himself no longer. 'What happened to the fucking *door of your car!*'

'So well you should ask that, Tom.' Mr Harmless swung his legs out of the bed, furious. 'There was this Land Rover...'

When Mr Harmless had finished telling the story, Tom Rooney could scarcely believe his ears. 'You mean — the door is still lying on the side of the road?'

Mr Harmless nodded. 'We couldn't lift it, you see?' He got to his feet and walked over to the wardrobe. 'But come on now, Tom, you and me will go back together and see if we can move it between us. Two *men* on the job, wha'?'

'Did you phone a garage or anything?'

'They were all shut. The hotel was going to ring one for us in the morning.'

*

It had started to rain.

By the time they reached the B4224, it was raining so hard Tom had to put his windscreen wipers on at full speed.

'Whereabouts?' he asked.

Mr Harmless was bent forward, peering through the windscreen. The B4224 was a country road about ten miles long, and it was pitch-dark. If it hadn't been for the car headlamps he wouldn't have been able to see anything at all.

'Well, now ... I'm not really sure...'

By daylight they were still driving up and down, searching; and the rain was still bucketing down.

And still no sign of the door.

As the morning got brighter, Mr Harmless was feeling exhausted. Tom Rooney had tears of frustrated rage in his eyes. *If I don't find that fucking door, Michael Lynch will...* Tom didn't know *what* Michael Lynch would do.

'Know what I think?' Mr Harmless suddenly said. 'I think with all this heavy rain ... I think the door must have slid down the bank, sometime in the night, and gone into the river.'

Chapter twelve

It was Breda's special day. She made her First Holy Communion in St Joseph's Church, and she looked beautiful in her white Communion dress, handmade in Italy. All the Lynch children were dressed smartly; the whole family turned out in great style.

The celebration dinner afterwards was held at the Enclave Hotel. The lawn outside the hotel was crowded with guests and little girls in white dresses.

Michael watched the various families milling around in groups, talking, while the First Communicants and their friends ran around squealing in general excitement.

Christine, slim, tall, and beautiful, looked very happy and relieved that the whole thing had passed off peacefully without any problems. But Michael's mother seemed to be complaining to her.

*

'Christine, there's no need for all this. I had sandwiches made back at the house.'

Christine felt a certain guilt. Mona Lynch had been looking forward to having everyone back to her house and packing it out with laughter and chat, but Christine was determined on having all the trimmings for Breda, and no expense spared.

She smiled at Mona. 'Michael wanted you to have a day out too.'

'But these restaurants are very dear.'

Mona had never lost her poverty mentality, and no matter how much money Michael gave her, which had been plenty over the years, she still believed — still *convinced* herself — that he was unemployed and living on welfare.

'They charge the earth, these hotel places. And you're waiting ages to get served.'

'Mam! Enjoy yourself!' Christine ordered.

Mona stared at her blankly for a moment, surprised and slightly baffled, as if Christine had asked her to do something totally foreign to her.

'Enjoy yourself!' Christine repeated. 'Breda wants to see you looking happy, Mam. And the sandwiches won't be wasted — Padraig and the others can eat them later on this evening.'

'That's true,' Mona half-heartedly agreed, but then her attention was diverted. 'Ah, there she is now! Doesn't she look just gorgeous!'

Both women gazed lovingly at the seven-year-old girl running across the lawn.

'Well, at least I can say she got her first prayer book from me,' Mona said with satisfaction.

*

'Da! Da!' Breda came running up to Michael. 'Look what Granny gave me.'

'What is it, chicken?'

'A holy book, with a gold cover and coloured pictures.'

She handed over the book for him to see. *My First Holy*

Communion Book. 'Oh, that's brilliant,' he said. 'What I'd give for a present like that!'

Breda's smile had a sweetness that touched Michael's heart.

He heard a shout and saw a neighbour waving.

'Look, there's Mrs Cassidy. Go on over, I think she might have something for you. I'll mind your book for you.'

Breda ran to receive a big hug and a kiss from Mrs Cassidy. Michael watched them chatting together excitedly as he took some twenty-pound notes from his pocket to slip them inside Breda's book.

The page he opened had a luridly mournful and blood-dripping illustration of the Crucifixion, which he disapproved of; it seemed wrong to him that small children should see pictures like that. Enough to give them nightmares.

As he closed the book, he noticed a car pulling up outside the entrance to the hotel. There was something familiar about the driver that caught his attention...

On the other side of the car, the passenger door opened and his brother Billy got out.

Billy looked pale and nervous. He walked round to the driver's window and began speaking to him intently, but the driver was looking across the grounds and indicated Breda.

Billy turned and called her.

'Uncle Billy!' Breda ran excitedly over to the car and showed off her beautiful new dress. And her white veil, which she flounced around her shoulders. And her new white shoes. And her new little white handbag.

Michael saw the driver smile and give Breda some money, talking to her as if he knew her well.

At that moment Padraig Lynch sidled up to Michael. 'All right there, son?'

Michael looked at his father.

Padraig's face, usually dour, was smiling cheerfully. 'It all went very nicely, I thought. Are we going inside for a drink?'

'Da, listen...' Michael nodded towards the driver of the car, who was still talking to Breda and Billy. 'Who is he? Should I know him?'

'I dunno...' Padraig Lynch shrugged. 'It's funny, though: he looks more like you than your brother does. Same hairdo an' all.'

That was true: the driver had his black hair cut short in the same style as Michael's, the shape of the face was almost the same, and the eyes were dark brown.

Michael narrowed his own eyes as he continued to watch. 'Why do I feel like I should know him?'

'Oh, hold on, I have him now!' Padraig snapped his fingers. 'He grew up around our way, all right. Went to college an' all after that. Higgins is his name. Ger ... Gerry ... no, *Jerome* Higgins. That's it. Jerome Higgins.'

Padraig dropped his voice and spoke out of the side of his mouth. 'He's in the IRA now, I heard.'

'IRA?' Michael arched an eyebrow disbelievingly; every petty thief these days claimed to be in the IRA.

'No, seriously,' Padraig insisted. 'I have it on the soundest information that Higgins went that way some years ago.'

'Da ... Da...' Breda ran up to Michael, delighted, holding up a five-pound note. 'Look what I got, Da.'

'Lucky old you.' He handed her the prayer book. 'Here you go. Mind that carefully, now.'

'Look, Granda...'

Michael glanced over at the car and saw Jerome Higgins squeeze Billy's arm in a matey way.

Why the hell would a fella from the IRA want to be so

friendly with Billy? It was nothing political, of that he was certain ... so it had to be something else. What?

'Are we going inside, son?'

'Yeah, Dad, we're going inside.' Michael turned and snapped a smile onto his face. 'Come on. Tony and his crowd will be waiting with their tongues hanging out.'

*

'Dead men don't talk,' Jerome Higgins said to Billy.

Billy's pale and nervous face had turned a greyish colour. 'What do you mean by that?'

'I never allow anyone to screw me twice. So if you try it once, that's it. Understand?'

Billy dropped his brow against the edge of the car roof and bit his lips together tightly, a grimace of pain moving over his face. 'Jesus, Higgins, I don't need a lecture or a warning, I need some painkillers.'

Jerome Higgins smiled sarcastically. 'Heroin and crack are not usually called painkillers. Have you tried aspirin?'

'Fuck's sake!' Billy hissed violently. 'Just give me the stuff!'

'And what will you give me?'

'Anything — anything you fucking want.'

'Not money. I'm not here to collect your debt. That's not the deal. You know what I want, Billy.'

'And you know what I fucking want. It's you that's screwing me up, Higgins. Are you dealing or not?'

'A two-thousand-pound-a-week habit is big money, Billy. And what was your cut from O'Donnell's? Fifty grand? Just enough to cover four or five months' supply. But I'm willing to do it cheap, much cheaper for you, Billy, on the condition that you deliver what I want.'

Billy's whole body was trembling now; his teeth were

on edge with anger. 'I thought the IRA were against drugs. I'm told up North they break the legs of pushers and give them punishment beatings for what they call antisocial behaviour.'

Billy's jaw was working overtime, his teeth now grinding in agony. 'Are you really IRA, Higgins, or are you just fucking me up with threats and false promises?'

'Nothing about me is false, Billy.'

'Then give me the stuff you fucking promised me!'

'Your medication?'

Higgins took a small packet from his pocket and slipped it to Billy. 'That should keep you going for a while. But remember, I've picked up your other debts, so you owe me, lots of dough, and —'

Billy didn't wait to listen to any more. He ran across the lawn and into the hotel and headed straight for the men's toilets and the privacy of a cubicle.

Fifteen minutes later he emerged a new man — relaxed and cheerful and ready to join his family in the celebrations.

*

Tony walked with Michael along the corridor from the hotel bar to the restaurant.

Tony seemed edgy, his eyes darting around all the time, as if he was waiting and watching out for someone who hadn't yet arrived.

At the restaurant doors, he finally took a breath and decided to come straight to the point. 'Listen, Michael ... you know that job Tom Rooney was doing for you in England?'

Something in Tony's voice made Michael look at him sharply. 'Yeah, what about it?'

Tony hesitated.

'Well, you see — that's it, you see, Michael... I always thought Tom Rooney was a bit of a fucking eejit, but I also thought he was sound, you know. If you had asked me, that's what I would have told you, that Tom was sound...'

Michael was looking darkly at him. 'Go on.'

'It looks like Tom's done a runner.'

'A runner?' Michael smiled. 'No way. Tom wouldn't do that. Because why the fuck would he think he could get away with it?'

Tony shrugged. 'It's not like him, I'll say that for him. But now I don't know. I'm beginning to wonder, can you ever trust anyone?'

'Yeah, you can. That's what it's all about. I wouldn't have let Tom do the job if I didn't trust him.'

'So what now?'

'Now you go find him. Bring him back.'

'Right.' Tony immediately turned away.

Michael caught his arm and gave him a wry grin. 'Tony, you can eat your dinner first.'

*

Inside the restaurant, they moved through a sea of white Communion dresses and packed tables decorated with pink roses and white carnations.

Suddenly Michael stopped in his tracks, alert. He was always alert. He had caught sight of a man standing at the far corner of the restaurant, outside the door of the toilets.

What the fuck is he doing here?

Although the man stood with his back to him, Michael would have recognised Detective Sergeant Noel Quigley from any angle.

His astonishment was so supreme, all he could do was

stand and stare. Was Noel Quigley following him? If he was, and this was Quigley's idea of covert surveillance, then he was doing it very badly.

A woman in her thirties and twin girls in Communion dresses came out of the ladies' toilets. The girls smiled up at Noel, who took a hand of each and led them towards the far exit door of the restaurant. Quigley with his wife and daughters; it was their Communion day too.

Michael relaxed.

Breda came running up to him, a wad of money in her hand. 'Da, look what everyone keeps giving me! Do you know how much I have now?'

'No matter how much it is, honeybunch, you're worth it.' He scooped Breda up and hugged her tightly. 'Because you're *my* little girl.'

*

It was after ten o'clock when they got back to the house. Christine had drunk more than a few glasses of wine and was slightly tipsy. Michael was still full of energy, always the night-owl.

Lisa looked drained. She had been very quiet all day, but no one had really noticed.

'I'll put the kettle on,' Christine said.

'No, I won't have any tea,' Lisa said, changing her mind. 'My head's splitting and I'm tired out. I think I'll just get the kids home to bed and fall in myself. Will you drive me, Michael?'

'Sure I will, Lisa.' He looked at her and frowned slightly. 'Are you feeling okay?'

'Yeah, just dead beat, that's all.'

Christine hugged her younger sister protectively. 'You look it, too. Flaked out. You'd better go. Michael will help you put the kids to bed.'

At the front door, Michael turned to Christine with a serious look on his face. 'Do you think I could have just one kiss, before I go?'

She laughed. 'You're mad, d'you know that?' She wrapped her arms around him and kissed him on the lips.

He looked into her eyes and smiled, and cuffed her lightly under the chin. 'Night, sweetheart.'

She watched him go to the car, half-turning for a last wave, and then he and Lisa were gone.

Christine felt not the slightest bit jealous. She had accepted the relationship between Michael and Lisa long ago. It did not detract from her marriage, because she knew Michael loved her above all others. They had been best friends since childhood, and their love for each other would always be deep and lasting. Not even his affair with Lisa could damage that.

Lisa was her youngest sister and her closest friend. When they had finally left the Mansions, Christine had been delighted when Lisa moved in with them. She was a great babysitter, and they had had lots of laughs, as well as sharing all their problems — until Lisa tearfully confessed her love for Michael, and Michael honestly confessed his love for both of them.

Strangely, Christine had known it would happen, and even understood. Michael was a warm and caring man, and devoted to his family. And Lisa had become part of his family. He had shown Lisa more care and kindness than anyone else had in her unprivileged life, so it was not surprising when Lisa fell in love with him.

All three had openly discussed their feelings. Michael had made no advances towards Lisa, because he believed in treating women with respect. No way could he ever cheat behind Christine's back; they had always trusted each other implicitly. And no way could he use Lisa just for sex, because he cared for her much more than that.

Christine knew that Michael was no womaniser — unlike some of his friends, who enjoyed getting off with other women behind their wives' backs. But Michael wasn't like that. He was a gentleman crook.

Yet Christine had known that this was a dilemma she would have to think about very carefully. She had always been devoted to Michael's happiness, and she didn't want Lisa banished from her life either; she loved her sister. Nor did Michael want to cause any hurt to Christine or their marriage.

Finally she had come up with an arrangement all three were happy with. It was better than cheating, better than jealousy and suspicions. And even if the arrangement was unorthodox and bizarre, Christine thought realistically, so was the rest of her life.

Ever since then, she and Lisa had shared their man, their pregnancies, their problems and their children — and, sure, it hadn't worked out too bad at all. Just one big family, staying loyal and sticking together, just like the old days in the Mansions.

*

Christine closed the front door and returned to the living-room. She snapped off the television. 'Come on, you lot, up to bed now. And no arguments.'

Breda didn't want to take off her lovely Communion dress. She begged to be let sleep in it.

Christine laughed and let her. 'All right, it's not as if you're ever going to be wearing it again.'

Tommy and Shane were asleep as soon as their heads touched the pillows.

In her own room, Christine kicked off her high-heeled shoes and sat on the bed, leaning back on her elbows. The day had gone well. She felt content.

Her eyes fixed on the poster on the wall. Caravaggio's *The Taking of Christ*. Was it a bit grim for a bedroom?

No, it wasn't. It was glorious art.

But then a thought struck her, and she began to chuckle to herself as she thought of the artist, Caravaggio. The more she read about him, the more she liked him.

In many ways she thought Caravaggio was just like Michael. He was very intelligent, was generously paid for his work, but his personality was alienated from the norm, and during his boyhood and most of his maturity he had scorned all official authority and been remarkably ill-behaved.

Yeah, just like Michael.

Although she hoped the similarity ended there — because Caravaggio had been killed when he was thirty-nine, and Michael was thirty-nine now.

Christine frowned, an uneasy feeling stirring in the pit of her stomach.

Chapter Thirteen

The following Saturday afternoon, Billy Lynch lay on the bed in his small flat in Rathmines and turned on the portable television. He hadn't eaten any breakfast or lunch and his stomach was empty, but he had just shot himself up in the bathroom and he was feeling good.

He could still feel some tension in his arm and leg muscles, but it would soon pass; it always did.

The rumpled bedsheet beneath him was dirty and stained with night sweat, but he didn't notice. The living-room and kitchen were in a worse state of disorder. Dirty dishes and plates of old food were scattered over the kitchen, and the living-room floor was covered in two-week-old newspapers.

An old Clint Eastwood movie was on the television. Billy stared at the screen but saw only a blur, his eyes iced with heroin. All the aches and pains were leaving his body, and his mind began to float inside a huge coloured balloon.

*

Tom Rooney wasn't feeling so good. He was sitting alone in a pub in England, feeling very sad and solitary.

He had been hiding out at a cousin's house in Birmingham's run-down Aston district, and he was still trying to make up his mind what he should do next. His eyes were abstracted and his lips constantly twisting together intently, as if he was pondering an insoluble problem.

He hated Birmingham — a real concrete jungle built for the industrial working class. There was no beauty in any of its buildings, few green parks, no quick journey out to the seafront, no lovely Georgian houses like those all around Dublin. And the people had an accent he could barely understand. Like the woman who lived next door to his cousin, who always seemed to be standing in her garden whenever Tom left the house, and who always insisted on speaking to him, as she had earlier that morning.

'We dane af av a laf las night, us lot did,' she had told him, a big happy grin on her pudding face, and he had nodded and grinned back, and was still trying to work out what the fuck she had said.

The pub was almost empty, dim and grim, and the beer was warm. Most of the men who packed the pub at night would be in the betting-shops now, gambling on the Saturday-afternoon race cards. Everyone in Birmingham seemed to love gambling — the men on horse racing and the women at Bingo.

Of course, there were the richer suburbs where the more well-to-do lived, but Tom didn't know any of them. So he was stuck here in Aston, like any Irish navvy, dreaming of home.

Tom longed to go back to Dublin, but he was too frightened. He prided himself on being a realist and knew he was far too cowardly to go back and face Michael Lynch and the consequences of messing up the gold deal.

And now even the fence in Manchester had become his enemy, believing that Tom had done the dirty on him and given 'the product' to another fence.

Tom sipped his warm beer and thought of Mr and Mrs

Harmless. If he ever went back to Dublin he would slash all the tyres on their car. He would break the radio aerial. He would piss in their petrol tank. He would phone them repeatedly in the middle of the night and keep waking them up from their sleep. He would annoy them something terrible for what they had done to him. And the most galling thing of all was that the two goofs didn't even *know* what they had done to him.

He consoled himself for a few minutes by plotting further vengeance on them if he ever went back. He would sneak into their house one night and poison their beloved cat. He would lodge a small bag of marbles down the pipe of their washing machine. He would —

'How're yeh, Tom?'

The accent was pure Dublin; it brought Tom back to life like a warm welcome.

He looked up at Tony Brady's granite face, and in a flash he understood that Tony had been sent to find him. He made no move to run, just shrugged his acceptance of the inevitable. Maybe he had even been waiting for it.

Two other men materialised beside Tony. They looked friendly enough, but they also spoke in Dublin accents as they greeted Tom like a regular acquaintance and sat down on either side of him.

Tony also sat down. He and Tom faced each other across the table. Tony Brady looked grave, almost reluctant to give a friend bad news.

'I've got to bring you back, Tom. There's half a million in gold to be accounted for. And only you can do that.'

Now the shock of Tony's appearance had sunk in, Tom Rooney began to feel a terrible fear.

'I did nothing wrong, Tony, I swear it. I'm innocent, but I know Michael won't believe it. You see, it was the old couple —'

'Don't be so frightened,' Tony said, his expression kindly. 'Just come back with us tonight, without any fuss or tricks, and you can explain it all to Michael.'

Tom nodded, his throat dry. He looked at each of the men. 'Will yous have a drink before we go?'

Tony shook his head. 'Sorry, Tom, we haven't time. We've got to drive from here up to Holyhead in time to catch the evening ferry.'

The two men stood up and went out the door of the pub first. Tom followed them, with Tony Brady behind him.

As Tom and Tony sat in the back seat of the car, Tom suddenly felt the fear again and looked plaintively at Tony.

'Tony, you and me have always been pals, haven't we?'

Tony nodded. 'We have, Tom.'

'So if Michael doesn't believe me, will you help me out? Please, Tony, will you try and get me off the hook?'

Tony looked at him with a reprimanding smile tinged with amusement, because getting Tom Rooney *on* the hook was what Michael Lynch intended to do.

*

Billy Lynch was feeling bad. His fix had worn off and his depression had come back worse than ever. He stood at the window and looked down at the street, beginning to darken now. Saturday night — a night for going out and having a good time. He felt too tired to even wash himself, let alone shave.

And he was almost broke.

Over the years he had always had plenty of money, from the robberies and the scams, but over the past six months he had blown it all away on smack and crack. His need for the stuff was getting voracious, unquenchable. Without it he couldn't think straight or feel right. Without it he couldn't enjoy anything. Not food, not drink, not women, not anything.

He turned back into the room and flopped down on the couch. He hated Jerome Higgins for screwing up his supply holes and taking over as his dealer. He hated Jerome Higgins for humiliating him, and for trying to use him to get to his brother.

Jerome Higgins had become like a constant sore tooth in his face. And yet, the one person Billy wanted to see at this minute was Jerome Higgins.

Billy leaned over to the coffee table, picked up the phone and tapped out the number of a mobile.

Jerome Higgins answered it.

Billy paused for a moment, a black wave of depression sweeping over him as he realised what he was now — no longer a self-governing man, but completely powerless.

'Hello, Jerome,' he said meekly.

*

At nine o'clock it had started to rain lightly. By eleven it was pouring down, but Michael, Lisa and Christine didn't seem to care as they came out of the Italian restaurant and made their way home arm in arm, singing raucously at the tops of their voices.

Now I need you more than I did before
And where I'll find comfort, God only knows.
But youuuu ... left me,
When I needed you most...

They turned in to their own road, too busy singing to notice the black BMW parked a few doors up from the house.

But youuuu ... left me, just when I needed you most...

The electric window of the car opened as they passed. A

voice spoke out to them.

'That's very nice ... Lisa and Christine, isn't it? Sorry, but I'm not sure which is which. Dark, you know.'

'Who's that?' Michael turned round.

Billy got out of the car and quickly walked up to Michael, his voice low. 'Michael, it's Jerome Higgins in the car. He wants to talk to you.'

'Jerome Higgins?' Michael eyed his brother warily. 'And since when have you become a messenger boy for the IRA, little fella?'

Higgins spoke from the open window. 'We've done a few favours for Billy.'

Michael looked at Billy's unkempt appearance and hunted eyes, and finally understood.

'Talk to him, will you,' Billy pleaded. 'A few minutes, that's all. Honestly. It's not trouble or anything... What's the problem?'

'I don't like being told what to do, that's the problem.'

'Please, Michael, just talk to him.'

Michael realised Billy was in trouble, bad trouble. He looked at Christine. Her answering look said, *Talk to him.*

'Wait here,' Michael said to the women. 'I won't be long.' He walked over to the window of the car.

Higgins got out of the car and spoke pleasantly. 'Glad our man Shay Kirby was able to be of help to you with that judge, Michael.'

'Shay isn't in the IRA any more.'

'Ah, but his training, Michael. His methods. '

'What do you want?'

'Well, I was just saying to Billy there, I think there could be a lot of merit in some co-operation between us.'

'Well, I don't.'

'Billy wouldn't agree with you, Michael. I suppose you know we had our eye on O'Donnell's Jewellery as well.'

'Tough shit.'

'So a reasonable cut from the two million would be a nice gesture to us, Michael. A reasonable cut, that's all. Call it ... a symbol of future collaboration.'

Michael's smile was full of disgust. 'A symbol of future fuck-all. You've neither the fucking brains nor the gumption to plan or do your own robbing, so you think you can squeeze an ordinary decent criminal who knows something about his job?'

He prodded a finger into Higgins's chest. 'Let me tell you something, Jerome. Fuck off and double fuck off. Got it?'

He turned away to rejoin the women.

A few seconds later he looked back, grinning. 'Hey, Higgins! No hard feelings, by the way. God loves a trier. And keep an eye on the newspapers, because that'll be the first time you hear about my next job — when it's all over the front pages. The biggest yet, way out of your league.'

As soon as they got inside the house, Christine looked at him anxiously. 'What job were you talking about?'

Michael shrugged. 'Don't ask me. I was just making it up as I went along. The fucker.'

*

The Saturday-night fun was over. Their moods were too deflated. Michael was too upset about Billy. He detested drugs, and he despised the dealers and pushers, especially now he knew they had caught his brother.

He stood in the kitchen, glowering with rage. Christine tried to calm him, but he was not to be appeased.

'It's what I say,' he insisted. 'Billy just couldn't stop himself fucking it up. Fucking up his whole life. And what is he now? A stoned bastard full of crack and smack and all that other shit he's either sniffing or shooting up. I wouldn't trust Billy now as far as I could throw him.'

He banged his fist furiously on the table. 'And you notice — you notice how none of them pushers ever touch the stuff themselves, they steer well clear of it themselves, the fucking bastards. Jesus, I knew Billy was a bit thick, but I didn't think he'd be stupid enough to get himself in hock to the IRA. And a man like Higgins, of all —'

Michael stopped talking, because he had suddenly remembered something. Something that made him want to be alone to think, to use his intelligence to puzzle this thing out.

He went to the corner room at the end of the hall and closed the door behind him. He sat down in his comfortable leather armchair and let his mind roam over the situation.

It had started some eight years ago, with the Dane brothers, who had given up robberies to move into the drug business because of the huge profits to be made. And it was less risky than holding up banks. Heroin being the most lucrative and highly addictive, they had pushed it the hardest, giving it out free at first, until even many of the kids in the schools were hopeless addicts, ready to do anything to get the money for a fix.

A few years later, out of desperation and necessity, the CPAD movement had been formed — Concerned Parents Against Drugs. And backing them to the hilt was the IRA.

A list of twenty named drug dealers operating in England and selling heroin to Irish pushers, believed to be an IRA hit list, had been sent to a national newspaper.

Within two years, twelve of the named English dealers had been either shot in cold blood or killed in mysterious circumstances. The Provos were quite happy to bomb and kill and finance their war in the North with robberies from Irish banks, but they refused to countenance the peddling of drugs, especially to children.

So that was it. Michael sat forward in his chair. Now he had sussed it out. Jerome Higgins had no great connections in the Provos backing him, just a few hired crooks posing as Provos. Michael was sure of it. Higgins was using the IRA name for his own personal gain, but he was nothing more than a maverick, a lone operator using the big political guns in the North as his threat to extort money from ordinary decent criminals down South.

The fucker.

Christine popped her head into the room. 'Someone's knocking on the front door,' she said. 'Will you go or shall I?'

Michael walked into the hall and listened. The knocking came again, a quiet and timid knocking — so it wasn't the gardaí, anyway.

He went to the door and opened it. Billy stood forlorn in the rain. He looked hopeless and helpless. He shrugged his shoulders and mumbled, 'I'm sorry, Michael.'

Michael gave him a cold stare, then spoke over his shoulder to Christine. 'Get me a few grand out of the box, Christine.'

Billy was rubbing his head.

'Were you just using, keeping it for yourself, or have you been dealing it as well?' Michael asked.

'Both,' Billy admitted lamely.

Michael's face was as Billy had never seen it before. The brown eyes had turned black and his face looked white.

'Then you can fuck off,' Michael snapped. 'I want you out of Dublin fast, little fella. England, Amsterdam, wherever. But keep away from Higgins and keep away from me.'

Christine handed Michael the cash. He handed it over to Billy. 'You hear? I want you out of Dublin fast.'

Billy nodded.

Michael slammed the door in his brother's rain-soaked face.

Chapter fourteen

Michael was certain Tom Rooney was lying, and he said so.

The cock-and-bull story of the old couple losing their car door was nothing but a load of crap that only an eejit like Tom Rooney would make up and think he could get away with.

Tom froze in terrified dismay.

They were in the warehouse, standing by an old car parked in a special bay where repairs were usually done. Tom glanced over his shoulder, as if desperately looking for some escape, but Tony and Stevie were standing right behind him.

Michael was sitting inside the car, on the back seat, his expression resolute and deadly as he stared through the open window of the car at Tom Rooney.

Tom felt a sudden weakness in his legs and started to sag. Stevie and Tony grabbed his arms and held him up.

'Put his hand where I want it,' Michael said quietly, opening the car door.

Tony and Stevie grabbed Tom's hand and placed it on the inner rim of the door.

'So, Tom, I'll ask you again: what did you do with the gold?'

When Tom gave no answer, Michael slammed the door hard onto the hand. Tom let out a scream of excruciating pain. '*I don't know!* Honestly, Michael...'

'Are you beginning to get the feeling, Tom, that I don't believe you?'

'Please, Michael, please, I *swear*...'

Michael, his face set, seemed not to hear. 'I mean, even if it's true that this old couple got their car door ripped off by a passing Land Rover and left it abandoned on the side of the road —'

'I searched, Michael, I drove up and down.'

'But you see, you didn't come back to tell me this straight away, did you, Tom?'

Michael opened the car door and slammed it again, violently. Tom squealed pathetically as one of his fingers broke.

'We risked a lot to get that gold, Tom. We risked years in prison to get that gold. All of us. And you think we're going to shrug our shoulders now and say, "Okay, pal, we believe your stupid story"?'

'It's the truth, Michael, the *truth*!'

Michael motioned to Stevie and Tony to move Tom back a few paces so he could get out of the car. He said quietly, 'You should have come back, Tom.'

'I was afraid. I'd fucked up and I was afraid.'

'So you don't think I'm a fair man, then, Tom?'

'No, Michael, it's not that —'

'*What did you do with the gold?*'

'Nothing... Oh, Jesus, Michael, I'm sorry. Please ... please.'

Michael turned his head and looked at the front of the car, which Stevie had got ready. Both the front windows were down. A chain had been passed through both windows and fitted onto a huge metal hook on a hoist.

'Hold his hands ready,' he said.

He shut the back door of the car, then leaned in through the open window and lifted out the seat-belt, which he wound tightly around Tom's wrist.

Tom whimpered, 'Oh God, I did nothing!'

Michael signalled to Stevie to set the machinery in motion.

'I never got the gold. It — it's gone. I'd do anything to get it back. You have to believe me!'

Stevie pushed the lever of the hoist, jerking the car and Tom high into the air. Tom screamed, trying to hold on for dear life as the hoist began to pull him and the car up towards the roof of the huge warehouse, to a height that would severely damage him, or even kill him, if he fell or was suddenly dropped.

Michael stood looking up at him.

'You ran away, Tom. Only scumbags run away. You can't trust someone who does that. Would you trust them, Tom? Would you?'

'N-n-no.'

'So you see why this is a problem we have to deal with, don't you? You didn't come back.' Michael looked upwards at Tom's legs kicking wildly. 'And I don't like to be left hanging around, Tom.'

'N-no.'

'So where's the gold!'

'I don't know!' Tom screamed. 'I don't knooow!'

Michael spoke quietly to Stevie and Tony. 'Leave him hanging there for a while, until he decides to tell us the truth.'

Tony Brady nodded. 'He must know the weight of his body will bring him down in the end.'

Michael smiled grimly. 'But he also knows that the truth will get him down sooner and safer. If he knows where the gold is, he'll tell us eventually — bet on it.'

But in the hour that followed, Tom Rooney had nothing to tell. He couldn't even think of some story to make up. All he knew was the truth, and he kept shouting it down to them.

'Why don't you go and ask the old couple... Oh Jesus, my arms are ripping off...'

Michael paused for a long moment. Doubts were creeping into his mind. He looked questioningly at Stevie and Tony.

'What do you think?'

Stevie shrugged. 'I don't know, Michael.'

Tony Brady was more forthright. 'I'd say — I mean, I'm not certain or anything, but I'm beginning to believe him.'

When Michael finally spoke, his voice held a dismissal. 'Yeah, I think you're right. The fucker is obviously innocent. His story is so stupid it's probably true.'

He nodded at Stevie. 'Okay, get him down.'

When Tom Rooney's feet finally touched the ground, he was so relieved he almost collapsed in gratitude at Michael's feet.

Michael's face showed no trace of emotion. If Tom's story was true, as it seemed to be, then the gold was lost and gone. A fluke, a ridiculous farce, a great find for some diver in the long stretch of the River Severn sometime in the years ahead, maybe never. Maybe the gold would stay lost for centuries. All they had now was the present, and the absurd failure of the plan.

But Michael believed in being fair. 'I was wrong about you, Tom,' he said. 'I believe your story now.'

'It's the truth, Michael — honestly, it's the truth.'

Michael nodded wearily. 'I know, Tom, and I'm sorry. Stevie and Tony will take you to the hospital to get that hand fixed up.'

He looked with some concern at Tom's blood-soaked hand. 'Are you on the medical card, by the way? I mean, this won't cost you anything, will it, Tom? The medical treatment?'

Tom Rooney shook his head, then stuttered, 'I — I'm on the card... N-no problems, Michael.'

'Grand.' Michael's smile was friendly. 'G'night, so.'

*

Inside the hospital waiting-lounge, Tom Rooney was feeling in great form. It was all over, and he was back home in Dublin, and a smashed hand was a doddle to suffer when he had been expecting to be killed at the very least.

As always, they were waiting ages to see a doctor. Tony and Stevie sat on either side of Tom on the bench and tried to keep his spirits up with a bit of black humour.

'Oh yes,' Stevie told Tom, 'we knew what Michael was planning to do with you when he asked us to *handle* it.'

'That's why he sent us here with you to the hospital,' Tony said. 'He thought you might need a hand.'

Tom Rooney laughed hilariously. What were a few broken fingers, when any other gang boss would have creamed him for losing half a million?

*

Michael Lynch couldn't get to sleep that night.

The small hours of the night had begun, but he was still awake, restless. He looked at Christine sleeping soundlessly beside him, lying on her stomach, one arm hanging over the side of the bed.

He turned onto his back and stared at the wall, knowing why he could not sleep. He was still grieving the loss of the gold from O'Donnell's.

What a *great* robbery that had been — planned to perfection, and carried out to perfection... But now it had all been spoiled by the loss of the gold.

If the rest of the criminal fraternity heard about it, he would be a laughing-stock. And of course no other gang would ever employ Tom Rooney after this, so he was stuck with him, if only to keep Tom's mouth shut.

Still, he forgave himself for trusting Tom. He was a fucking eejit, but he had always been sound in every other way. The plan had just gone wrong, and Tom was as much a victim of it as himself. Two victims of a wicked world that allowed posh country fecks in a Land Rover to speed faster than the limit, losing ordinary decent criminals a door full of gold.

Sickening.

He looked at the clock on the bedside locker and turned with a heavy sigh onto his stomach, tucking his arms under the pillow. Some sleep was what he needed now.

An hour later, he turned onto his back and sighed again. Dawn was breaking, and its light misted the room in a bluey-grey colour.

His eyes moved around the room as his thoughts searched for somewhere to land. Should he get up and watch some television to make him drowsy, or stay where he was and make one last effort to sleep?

His gaze rested on the poster of Caravaggio's master-piece, *The Taking of Christ*. The colours were not so vivid in the dawn light, the background was dark and blurry; only the face of Jesus was clear, still sorrowful and mournful, still resigned to his fate.

He wished Christine would take the poster down. It was beginning to give him the woes. God knew why anyone would want to pay thirty million pounds for the original. Wasn't that what Christine had said the original painting in the National Gallery had been valued at — around thirty million?

He stared at the poster with greater interest. His heart was beginning to pound in the way it always did when a plan was coming to him. His excitement intensified until all desire for sleep vanished.

He leaned over and shook Christine. 'Wake up, love, I've something to ask you.' He shook her again. 'Come on, Christine, wake up.'

'Ah, Michael, stop,' she murmured, half-asleep. She turned over and blinked at him.

'Christine, will you do me a big favour?'

'No, I'm too tired, love.'

'Will you teach me something about art?'

'Now?'

'How sleepy are you?'

'Very sleepy.'

He shrugged. 'Okay, then, tomorrów will do fine.'

'Tomorrow — ah, grand...' Christine yawned. She turned over again, pulling the duvet warmly around her.

A few minutes later, Christine's eyes popped open. '*Art*, did you say?'

She flipped over to stare at him pulling on his clothes. 'Why d'you want to learn about art?'

But Michael was already out the bedroom door, almost singing to himself as he headed down the stairs to make himself a cup of coffee and work out his plan. And a *master* of a plan it would be. A fucking dream come true! And, shit, he deserved it.

Chapter Fifteen

The Dublin streets were darkening. It had been a long and claustrophobic day for Michael, but now, on his walk to Merrion Square, he began to enjoy the sights and sounds of his own city.

He had spent the entire morning in the little corner room, working on his plan, scribbling notes and making phone calls to tourist agencies and window glazers, using a different false name in each case.

Christine kept interrupting him, popping her head round the door and asking what he wanted to know about art. She seemed amused and curious, but her interruptions had begun to annoy him.

Finally he told her that he had changed his mind, didn't want to know anything about art, and was going to have a bath instead. He locked himself in the bathroom so he could continue his planning in peace.

He had soaked in the hot bath for over half an hour, enjoying the pleasant scent as he daydreamed of great riches. All along the edge of the tub was a collection of jars and bottles containing Christine's bath salts and aromatherapy bath oils. He dropped a measure from each one into the bathwater and luxuriated in the steamy scent. It was a rich scent. It reminded him of the only time he had stayed overnight in a posh hotel, on his honeymoon. The Gresham Hotel in O'Connell Street. In the en-suite bathroom there had been a basket containing an assortment of fancy soaps, and he had sat in the bath and used every one, to get his money's worth.

When he got out of the bath he could feel all the tiredness had been soothed out of his muscles. He felt as refreshed and energetic as an athlete on his way to the Olympics. He dried his body and wished he didn't have so much black hair on his chest — although he would have liked a bit more hair on his head. He stared in the mirror and closely inspected his hairline; it was definitely receding a bit.

He continued thinking about his master plan as he shaved. For this particular operation, he had decided to stick to his old and trusted methods. Experience had taught him time and time again that the best and most successful plans were always very simple — nothing complex or fancy.

The kids had put a halt to his daydreaming, coming in from school and charging up the stairs, banging on the bathroom door and demanding to be let in. He had sighed and got dressed. No rest for the wicked.

When he had come out of the bathroom, all spruced up and smelling of bath oils, Christine had sniffed him suspiciously.

'Are you getting vain, or what?'

He looked at her and grinned. 'Yeah, and I might go out later and try to get a suntan.'

*

But it was almost night when he drove his car into the city centre. He parked near Merrion Square and walked to the National Gallery, viewing its outer structure like an interested tourist. Tomorrow he would take the next step and ask Christine to accompany him *inside* the gallery.

He turned and strolled back to his car, but on a sudden impulse he turned away and decided to take a stroll through the city.

Dublin had become the new place for tourists looking for a good time and usually getting it. The Irish had always loved visitors and usually welcomed them with good-humoured charm. It was now a city he would not have recognised from the days of his youth, filled with voices speaking in languages he did not understand — Germans, Dutch people, and of course hordes of Scandinavians. But then, Dublin was a Viking city, so maybe that was why the Scandinavians liked it so much.

And Americans — always loads of Irish-Americans, home to find their roots.

Americans — of course! What a great idea to use in his plan! He smiled and paused for a moment to congratulate himself on the beautiful banality of his scheming.

He walked on towards the quays. It was Friday night, so the tourists were out in force, the older ones sauntering up towards the famous O'Connell Street and Flanagan's Restaurant for a good American steak supper, while the younger ones headed towards the clubs and wherever the neon lights beckoned.

His mind kept working while his legs took him all over the place, on one of the longest walks he had ever taken.

On Leeson Street he had entered Dublin's famous nightclub zone, but it was a hot-dog stall that attracted his interest. The night air was fresh, and the smell of hot dogs and hamburgers and frying onions made him hungry.

He wandered up to the stall, ordered a hot dog laced with onions and mustard, and ate it standing alongside the counter. It was so delicious he ordered another two, chewing as he stood looking around him. This street, he knew, would be crowded by midnight, the doorways packed with people trying to get into the clubs.

He polished off the last of his hot dogs and wiped his hands on the paper napkin. Time to go home. He had thought out a good amount of his plan, and that was enough for today.

Yet on the drive home he could still feel some exhilaration lingering, some excitement still buzzing in his mind at the thought of the job ahead.

And *that*, he realised, was the main downfall of the gardaí, who went about their work using only half their brains. They plodded around in the serious belief that all criminals devised their plans and carried out robberies for the sole purpose of netting money.

But that was only the half of it — the loot and the profit. The other half was the thrill and *enjoyment* of it all. The real *fun* of the robbers fucking the cops, of winning the game against all the odds.

He was still grinning to himself when he entered the house and met Christine's worried stare.

'Michael,' she exclaimed, 'where have you *been*?'

'To the National Gallery.'

'What for?'

'To look at it.'

'But it's closed.'

'I know that. But I thought you and me could maybe go there tomorrow, when it's open.'

The suspicious look was back in Christine's eyes. 'Michael, are you scheming up something?'

'Pillow talk,' Michael said tiredly. 'I had no sleep last night, remember. And now I'm jaded. So if you want to know what's on, I'll tell you all about it in bed.'

Chapter Sixteen

The Caravaggio Exhibition at the National Gallery of Ireland was still drawing great crowds.

Michael and Christine looked like any other art-loving couple as they joined the long queue of people waiting outside. Christine knew all about Caravaggio now, having studied him thoroughly.

'Mostly he did religious paintings,' she said to Michael, 'but only because that's where the money was in those days. Cardinals and bishops were always hiring artists to paint scenes from the Bible.'

Michael was noting the video cameras at each end of the building.

'And lords, of course — they were always commissioning religious paintings, too,' Christine continued. 'Lords of the manor trying to show off how holy they were.'

The queue moved at a snail's pace, but finally they were inside the main door of the National Gallery and walking along the corridor.

'Caravaggio had to do a runner out of Rome after he killed a man in a fight,' Christine said. 'He was a bit of a headcase, you know.'

Again Michael was noting the video cameras, the width of the corridor, and the ushers positioned at all entrances.

Finally they arrived at the large, light room where *The Taking of Christ* was displayed.

Other paintings in the collection were hung strategically around the walls, but Michael was interested in only one. He stood staring at the face of Jesus, as if transfixed.

'You see there — Jesus and Judas?' Christine whispered. 'Caravaggio just used fellas off the street as his models. He was always hanging around bars and whorehouses; then he'd pick out someone who looked interesting to be his Jesus or whoever.'

She smiled. 'I think he got a big kick out of that. Having cardinals on their knees praying away to a painting of a murderer or something.'

Michael's eyes were still fixed on Jesus. In his mind's eye, the face of Jesus was slowly turning into his own face — hounded, persecuted... His gaze moved across to the face of Judas, sly and treacherous ... and there he saw Jerome Higgins.

At the far right of the painting was a third figure, standing with the soldiers; a man holding a lamp, pretending to be a good man ... Detective Sergeant Noel Quigley himself.

'That fella in the corner,' Christine said, 'that's Caravaggio, a self-portrait.'

Michael grinned at his little fantasy.

Christine nudged him. 'What are you laughing at?'

'Oh, nothing.' Michael shrugged. 'I was just thinking, you know, about what lasts, and who gets the benefit.'

'What d'you mean?'

'I mean, your man who painted this. Caravaggio. He did all the work but never got the money. Just got himself run out of town and bumped off. Oh, sure, he's got the reputation, all right, and everyone thinks he's great, and so on; but he never saw any of the money that painting's supposed to be worth, did he? So I mean, like — what's the fucking point, then?'

'Are you afraid no one will remember you after you're dead? And, by the way, I think you *should* take up painting.'

'What — just so I'll be remembered?'

Christine smirked. 'No, so you can do the kitchen. It needs a few new coats.'

*

The Jesuit Community House was large and well-kept, a Georgian town house with gleaming-clean windows, and the garden in front was lovingly cared for.

'Cleanliness is next to godliness,' Michael smiled.

Christine led the way up the stone steps and rapped the brass knocker. A minute later the door was opened by an old priest, who spontaneously smiled at them.

'Hello, yes?'

Christine and Michael smiled back. 'Father Grogan?' Christine asked.

'Paul Grogan, yes, that's me.'

'My name is Christine. I phoned you about the Caravaggio.'

'Oh, yes! Of course.' He opened the door wider. 'Come in. Welcome.'

Father Grogan led the way down a flight of stairs into the basement refectory — a spacious room with a long wooden table down its centre, the wood vigorously polished to a beautiful shine.

'Now the masterpiece was hanging right there for years.' Father Grogan pointed to a painting hanging on the wall at the far end of the room. 'Just hanging there, looking down at everyone eating their supper, and no one took any notice of it. Getting dirtier and dirtier, it was. Then one day I was celebrating mass in our little chapel upstairs, and the reading that morning was Luke's wonderfully moving account of Veronica washing the face of Jesus, and I suddenly thought, "We must have that beautiful painting cleaned." No idea what was about to be uncovered: a *Caravaggio*! A priceless original.'

Father Grogan smiled again, sadly. 'It was a pity for us, of course, in a way, because it was lovely to have it hanging there. But, well ... as soon as we knew its value, we all realised it couldn't stay here.'

He laughed. 'I mean, any half-decent thief could just walk in — although it hasn't happened so far, touch wood. The gallery made us that very fine copy, though.'

The three of them were now standing in front of the copy. To Michael it looked identical in every way to the original he had seen in the gallery.

He was looking measuringly at the canvas. 'Same size and all, yeah?'

'Oh yes, an absolute replica,' Father Grogan replied. 'I couldn't tell the difference.'

'I couldn't either,' Christine said.

'What about an art expert?' Michael asked.

Christine shot Michael a quick look of warning, but Michael had astutely realised that Father Grogan was a true innocent who saw good in everyone.

'An art expert? Ah well, now he — or she — would spot it in seconds. Apparently there's about half a dozen immediate visual clues.' The priest smiled at Christine. 'You've probably learned all about them yourself, Christine, for your research.'

'Yes, yes. That's right.' She laughed lightly, looking slightly embarrassed. 'But I haven't really started work on that part of it yet.'

Michael was genuinely puzzled. 'But if it's really worth thirty million, why didn't you sell it to the National Gallery, instead of giving it to them?'

'Good question,' Father Grogan agreed. 'Well, not blowing our own trumpets, now, but I suppose we just thought it was the right thing to do.'

Michael stood looking at the priest, very impressed.

'Thank you, Father,' Christine said, 'for taking the time to show me the painting. It's very good of you.'

'Ah, not at all.' The priest smiled happily. 'Now come on and I'll show you our little chapel.'

As they left the refectory, Michael's eyes sized up the room, especially the window looking out on the back yard.

*

Six days later, a large minibus, with the name 'RAFFERTY'S TOURS' emblazoned across the front, pulled up and parked in a prime spot allocated for group tours outside the National Gallery. On the side of the bus was the slogan, *We'll give you the run-around.*

A group of stereotypical American tourists disembarked and joined the queue. Loud clothes, baseball caps, golfing hats and sunglasses effectively hid their faces — Michael Lynch and his gang of criminals in a simple, if tasteless, disguise.

Michael was the last to disembark; at the door of the bus he paused, turned back to the driver of Rafferty's Tours, and spoke with a believable American accent.

'I don't think we're gonna do more than ten minutes here; we've still gotta helluva lot more sightseeing to do. So stand by ready for us, would you, pal?'

'Yeah, sure — no problem.'

The group moved as a block into the gallery, following

the crowd into the room that housed *The Taking of Christ*. They spread out around the room, pretending to look at the other paintings hanging on the walls, but each covertly watched Michael, waiting for the signal.

Only Tony stayed by Michael's side, both standing directly in front of *The Taking of Christ*.

Tony suddenly turned and kissed Michael's cheek — just as Judas is doing to Christ in the painting: *the signal*.

Immediately, all the gang moved to the paintings on the walls in front of them and began to lift them down.

Alarms screeched. All the other visitors in the crowd looked on, aghast, nervous and not quite knowing what to do. Michael and Tony had already stepped forward and lifted down *The Taking of Christ*.

More alarm sirens screamed.

A number of the ushers rushed forward. They stopped dead in their tracks as the rest of the gang speedily moved to form a circle around Michael and Tony, while holding their various paintings in front of them like protective shields — precious works of priceless art that no usher would risk damaging under any circumstances.

Stevie Brady and Shay Kirby produced guns and fired into the air. The crowd began to scream, the ushers backed away.

The gang began driving towards them, inside their circle of paintings.

Seconds later they were in the corridor, rushing down it, alarm bells still ringing madly. A group of security men had gathered to try and stop them, but once again the presence of guns and the danger of damaging the works of art made them hold back.

The circle moved towards the front door. Once outside, the gang broke formation and ran backwards to the minibus, still gripping their paintings as shields, held towards the security men who were now crowding out of the main entrance.

The waiting driver was staring in shock at the commotion. A second later he was grabbed by Alec Duignan and violently hurled out of the bus. Michael and the others piled in.

Alec expertly palmed the gears and gunned the engine, and the minibus zoomed away.

It had taken less than ten minutes to pull off the second-biggest art robbery in the world.

*

The police had already been alerted; the gallery's alarm system was connected to Garda Headquarters.

'Merrion Square,' police-car radios were informed. *'Rafferty's Tours minibus speeding towards Merrion Square. All units proceed and assist.'*

The minibus turned the corner and screeched around Merrion Square. Two squad cars were immediately on its tail.

Michael was sitting near the back door of the bus, watching intently through the window as the squad cars began to close in. He had planned for all possible eventualities, and he now nodded at Stevie, who promptly picked up a painting of a nude and waited.

'The first is closing in and armed,' Michael said.

A detective marksman leaned out of the window of the first squad car with a rifle in his hands.

'Now, Stevie!'

As the marksman prepared to fire, Michael pushed open the back door of the bus, and Stevie hung the painting out, making sure the detective saw it, before dropping it down on the road. Instantly the driver of the squad car braked and swerved to avoid destroying the work of art.

'See that?' Michael said with a grin. 'I knew we were a country that respected art.'

The minibus sped on.

*

When they reached the Hubband Bridge area, Michael sat in the minibus camouflaging the masterpiece — fitting a square of mirrored glass into the frame, neatly covering the Caravaggio.

The bus swung into a lane near the canal and stopped. Every man jumped out, except Shay Kirby, who paused just long enough to set a small explosive to a timer.

'Two minutes,' Shay yelled, springing down and running over to the car Alec had geared up and running.

Michael didn't get into the car with the others. He carried *The Taking of Christ*, now concealed by the mirror, and attached it to the outside of a small van bearing the name 'OLD MASTERS GLAZING COMPANY' and, running underneath, the tag line: *We help you see through everything*.

He got in behind the wheel and backed the van carefully out of the lane, reversing onto the main road and driving away a second before the explosion destroyed the minibus.

Chapter Seventeen

6.09 in the morning.

The dawn was brightening, the birds were chirping, but most people were still in their beds asleep.

In the little chapel inside the Jesuit Community House, Father Grogan was standing with his back to the window, facing the altar. His blue eyes were fixed on the Gospel of Matthew, his hands held out in prayer, his words a melodious chant.

'The night before He suffered, He took bread and gave thanks and praise...'

Nine other priests knelt with heads bowed as Father Grogan celebrated morning mass.

'He broke the bread, and gave it to His disciples...'

If Father Grogan had turned around and looked through the window behind him, he might have seen Michael Lynch in the garden below, walking towards the back door of the house as if he was a delivery man, carrying a wooden-framed mirror.

'Take this, all of you, and eat...'

The back door leading into the basement refectory was directly below the room where mass was being celebrated. Michael broke into the house easily and quietly, closing the door behind him. He could faintly hear sounds from the mass upstairs, and he knew he would have at least twenty minutes safe from interruption.

The refectory looked different from when he had last seen it; less sparse, and more homely. There was still a sparkling shine on the rich brown of the long table, but now it was set for breakfast with white cups and saucers and gleaming white plates.

Two sconces of white light hung down from the ceiling, highlighting the table and two large baskets of golden bread-rolls, heavy with flour. He could smell the freshness of the bread-rolls, as if they hadn't long come out of the oven. His eyes moved over the dishes of rich yellow butter, and the platters of cheese so fresh that blisters of milk were still oozing from its waxen skin.

On the far right of the refectory was an open door that led to a small kitchen. He knew it was a kitchen because of the smell of bacon coming from it, but he also knew that the priest who did the cooking would be upstairs with the others, celebrating morning mass.

He moved swiftly through the room, took down the replica of *The Taking of Christ*, and replaced it with Caravaggio's original, grinning as he hung the master-piece back on the wall.

'Alleluia! Alleluia!...'

He stood back to check that everything was as it should be. Then he fitted the mirror over the framed replica and lifted it with both hands, walked out of the refectory, and left the house as quietly as he had entered it, closing the back door silently behind him.

Upstairs, Father Grogan was concluding the mass. 'Thank you, Lord, for the gifts you have bestowed on us, your unworthy servants...'

*

Tom Rooney had recovered from his ordeal. His right hand was still damaged and he would probably never be able to pick a lock again, but he had been able to lift down and hold up a painting in the National Gallery, playing his part in the robbery as well as any of the others, and he was still one of the gang.

Tom was very relieved about that. A criminal's gang was a criminal's second family. And in Tom's opinion, the gang he belonged to was the best in Ireland, maybe even the world. And it stayed the best because the boss vehemently insisted on one rule — *Stay loyal, and stick together.*

Tom was feeling good when he made his way out to the Pigeon House, later that night, to meet the others. There he met up with Stevie and Tony and Alec and the boss man himself.

Michael was in high form when he unlocked the doors of the warehouse and grinned at his men. 'Never mind if there *are* bastards out there trying to grind you down, keep you poor, and put you away. They don't count. Not with us. We'll just carry on giving them the run-around.'

They all laughed as they followed him up the stairs to his darkened office. 'And I've got a nice surprise in here to show you,' Michael added.

He unlocked the office door and pushed it open. 'For your eyes only, lads. Wait till you see this.'

He switched on the light.

The Taking of Christ hung on the far wall, surrounded by press cuttings with huge headlines about the robbery. The entire wall was covered with newspaper headlines.

The men whooped and cheered.

Michael grinned. 'Every newspaper in the country, and most of the Brit papers too. And none of them have a fucking clue who did it!'

He closed the door behind the men and locked it. 'Do yous want to see some of the TV reports? I have a tape there, all ready.'

The old television set he kept in the office had been moved to stand directly under *The Taking of Christ*. A video recorder was placed beside the TV.

Michael switched on the tape.

The screen blazed to life. Shaky handheld shots of Michael leaving the unemployment office ... leaving court, hooded... TV crews pursuing his car... Detective Sergeant Noel Quigley standing on the steps of the Four Courts after the acquittal, his face fuming as a reporter questioned him.

'... But the more you hound him, the more ordinary people seem to think he's a great laugh.'

Quigley looked disgusted.

'I think events have shown that Michael Lynch's jokes are not very funny. He thinks he can have a laugh at the whole country's expense. Well, not any more.'

'Can't I?' Michael sneered at the screen. 'You've still got no results, have you, Quigley? And not a fucking clue it was me who did the art job, yeh stupid prick.'

He fast-forwarded the tape to reports of the art theft. Shots of the National Gallery of Ireland, a huge sign announcing the Caravaggio Exhibition... The room empty of all its canvases... Video surveillance shots, from inside the gallery, of a group of American tourists in baseball caps and sunglasses carrying out the paintings in a grouped circle, two of them visibly armed with guns...

But the pundits speaking on TV were quite certain the thieves were not Americans, but an international gang of art experts — possibly even a gang known to Interpol.

'Feckin' eejits.' Michael switched off the tape. 'Oh, and by the way, lads, you know this thing about me becoming

a bit of a TV star lately? Well, I want you all to know —'
He took out a large pair of sunglasses and put them on.
'— that it's not going to change me one little bit!'

Everyone laughed except Stevie, who stood there in
his denims looking worried, his eyes on the painting. 'So
how are we getting rid of it, Michael?'

'Oh, it's all sussed,' Michael replied confidently. 'Alec
is going to Amsterdam next week to check out this fence
I've been told about. A specialist.'

'Can I just say —' Tony was smiling as he threw his
arm around Michael. 'Can I just say that this man — and
I've known him a lot longer than any of you fuckers —
this man is a genius. Right?'

'Right!'

'And it's thanks to him,' Tony continued sincerely, 'it's
because of him that me and yous are ... whatever we are.
Put it all down to him — the laughs, the scams —'

'And the *money*!' Stevie laughed.

'Exactly!' Tony agreed. 'So, Michael — Boss Man — any
idea how much money we'll get for this holy picture here?'

Stevie nodded. 'Yeah; like, just because it's valued at
thirty million doesn't mean we'll get that.'

'We'll get enough to be rich, don't worry,' Michael said
confidently. 'And we've won; that's the point. See this?'
He pointed to all the newspaper headlines on the wall.
'See all this? Think about what it means. We're Number
One — not the gardaí, not the IRA, and not anyone else.
The whole country is in awe of us. We're bigger than
Riverdance! We're fucking superstars! Thanks to Himself
there...'

They all looked at *The Taking of Christ*.

But they'll never take me, Michael thought, a self-
assured smile on his face.

Chapter Eighteen

In Garda Headquarters, Detective Sergeant Noel Quigley was also watching a videotape: the security video from the National Gallery. He was showing it to Commissioner Daly and other officers.

'Look at those two there...' He pointed at two men standing directly in front of *The Taking of Christ*. 'Watch ... I think this is the signal.'

All the officers watched keenly as one of the men turned to the other and kissed his face. Immediately the rest of the gang members reached to lift down their paintings.

'You see — when he does that, everybody moves. The timing is spot-on. But it's the signal itself that caught me. You see what he's doing, sir?'

They watched the moment again. Noel froze it. Commissioner Daly looked at the other officers, bemused.

'Yes, you're right, he's giving a signal,' Daly said to Quigley. 'But I don't —'

'He's imitating the painting, sir. Look — the same as Judas.' Noel pointed to Jesus and Judas in the painting — then pointed to Michael and Tony.

Commissioner Daly nodded admiringly. 'Oh, yes, *very* clever!' He suddenly realised he was admiring the actions of a criminal. 'Well, what I mean —'

'It's very smart,' Noel agreed. 'Obviously someone who likes a joke. That's what made me realise — it's Michael Lynch.'

'What? Ah, Noel...' Commissioner Daly was getting tired of Quigley's obsession with Michael Lynch. Of course, the villain was becoming a very sore thorn in the flesh of the gardaí — but to finger him for this was just ridiculous.

Noel had read the Commissioner's expression, but he fought on. 'Sir, I know we can't make a positive ID from *this* picture. But look...'

On screen appeared a number of computer-enhanced images, comparing the figures of the two men in the art gallery with photographs of Michael Lynch and Tony Brady.

'I've had body-size and shape comparisons made with the photos of Lynch and Brady,' Noel said. 'Size of heads, height, everything. And they match.'

'And they may well match with a thousand other men in the country, too,' Daly said, slightly exasperated. 'But this is mere coincidence. Your nose alone should tell you Lynch isn't capable of this kind of thing.'

'No, sir, not coincidence,' Quigley insisted. 'I went back over all the security tapes since the Caravaggio Exhibition opened, and I found this.'

Noel lifted a tape and inserted it, pressed Play... Scenes of the Caravaggio room on an ordinary day. Noel froze a frame and pointed at two figures, then zoomed in on them.

'Michael Lynch and his wife Christine, on a day out.'

Commissioner Daly said, 'My wife also went to view the Caravaggio Exhibition, but it doesn't mean she was planning a robbery.'

'I know,' Noel conceded, 'I know it's not evidence of

anything. But what is *Lynch* doing there?'

'Accompanying his wife, perhaps?'

Noel Quigley shook his head. 'No, sir, I'm certain he went there for another reason.'

Commissioner Daly wasn't buying it. 'No, I'm sorry, I cannot agree. We'd look like fools if we presented this to the top lads from Interpol. These art robberies are the preserve of a few European gangs — Germans, Dutchmen. Art thieves who really know their business. Come on, Noel, admit it — Lynch is just not in their league.'

Noel turned away and lost himself in a silence, frustrated and angry. How Daly had risen through the ranks to Commissioner, he could not even start to comprehend. The man was a fool, a thick, and clearly not up to the job. Daly had no imagination, no initiative, and no real intelligence; why the high command had decided to promote a man with such limitations was simply beyond him.

Perhaps Daly gave the secret handshake or something? Had the Freemasons got into the gardaí?

Noel wondered.

Daly said, 'I think we ought to confer with Interpol.'

*

The gentleman from Interpol, Mr Jan De Heer, was very polished and very knowledgeable, especially about art thefts.

Commissioner Daly and Detective Sergeant Quigley listened to his opinion.

'It is certainly not the MO of any gang that we know. Which suggests to us, quite strongly, that it's a very clever local Irish operation, and the painting is still somewhere in your country. But you have probably come to that conclusion yourselves.'

Noel sat impassive.

Commissioner Daly quickly improvised. 'Ah, yes, yes indeed...' Daly decided not to look at Noel as he continued, 'Yes, well, of course we are pretty confident at this stage that it's the work of a gang led by Michael Lynch. I am personally familiar with Lynch's *modus operandi*, and although art theft isn't normally his thing, this particular robbery seems to have his mark on it, all right.'

Noel found Daly's audacity breathtaking.

'Good. If you know who it is you are dealing with, it will make a recovery operation much easier,' said De Heer. 'May I offer some further information, and perhaps some suggestions?'

Commissioner Daly beamed. 'Absolutely! Feel free.'

'We know that someone here in Dublin has made contact with a fence in Amsterdam,' said De Heer. 'I cannot divulge his real name, so let us call him Peter for now. Peter has made contact with us and has offered his co-operation ... for a fee, naturally.'

Noel said bluntly, 'So this Peter is a snout, right?'

*

A week later, Peter flew to Dublin from Amsterdam. He checked into his hotel and immediately rang room service and ordered a bottle of Dom Perignon champagne.

Peter was a crook and a natural-born scam-artist. He loved fine wines and good food, and he preferred living in luxury hotels, where he usually ordered the best on the menu from room service, ate the most expensive meals in the dining-room, and availed himself of every facility the hotel offered — then, a day before he was officially due to leave, slipped out of the hotel without paying the bill.

He had pulled this scam in hotels all over the world and had always got away with it, using false names and fake passports. Never once had he tipped a waiter or a bartender; he always apologised and explained shyly that he 'never carried cash'. And so everyone presumed that he must of course be extremely rich. Because it was common knowledge that the seriously rich never did carry cash.

His appearance was a natural asset to his deceptions. He always dressed in Armani suits, silk shirts, solid-gold cufflinks, and the final touch — designer gold-rimmed spectacles that made him look like a young Dutch lawyer or banker.

Peter had lost all moral scruples about deceiving people. His sophisticated brazenness and refined audacity knew no limits. In Amsterdam and Rotterdam, he had often tried to persuade high-class call-girls to accept payment by credit card or cheque — because, of course, being so rich, he 'never carried cash'. Any girl who refused was immediately charmed and cajoled and promised a gift of a brand-new car which he would personally deliver to her the following day, or a new luxury apartment which she could choose herself at his expense. He even promised one her own hotel, but in the end all any girl got was screwed.

Peter was always broke, and now he was in trouble with the Dutch police. But, having been brought up by rich parents in a life of drowsy luxury — before they had kicked him out — Peter knew a great deal about genuine art. And now he had agreed to help the police in an operation to catch the Irish art thieves, in return for a clean record and a payment of twenty-five thousand pounds.

He had jumped at the offer. He loved the idea of

pulling off such a sting, and one so easy; all of Holland had heard of the Caravaggio theft, and the man who had organised it was also reputed to be famous for performing amusing spoofs against the police. A man who enjoyed outrageous buffoonery. A small-time Irish crook who thought he could outwit even Interpol.

Peter smiled condescendingly. Only a high-rolling professional like himself was actually capable of that.

Then Peter remembered something else: this Michael Lynch was also reputed to be a fucking lunatic.

*

Michael was eager to meet the fence from Amsterdam. Eager to hear the price he would offer for the Caravaggio.

Peter telephoned Alec and suggested that the meeting with his boss should take place in a Chinese restaurant on South Great George's Street. The manager of the hotel had recommended it as the best in Dublin. And, after all, they would have a lot of talking to do; so why not enjoy some exquisite Oriental food at the same time?

Alec returned the call ten minutes later. 'Okay, the Chinese restaurant at eight o'clock. We'll see you inside.'

Peter decided to ring room service and then relax for a few hours, take a nap. He ordered a bottle of red wine, smoked salmon and a Caesar salad.

After he had eaten, Peter rang his contact in the Dutch police, then telephoned Commissioner Daly in Harcourt Square.

Commissioner Daly had been waiting for the call. This was his operation and he wanted a good result. An operations team of four men and two women had been detailed for covert surveillance of the meeting.

'Right, two of our men will be parked in a car nearby,

watching the entrance to the restaurant. Four others will be inside, two men and two women, in pairs, posing as ordinary couples out for an evening meal.'

'When will you move in?' Peter asked.

'Not in the restaurant,' Daly replied. 'We can't touch Lynch until we actually *see* him in possession of the Caravaggio. So your job is to make sure he takes you to wherever the painting is hidden. You'll have to pretend to authenticate it for your client before you agree on a price. We'll be watching you at all times, and once the painting is produced, then we'll move in and nab him.'

'Good.' Peter put down the phone and looked at his watch. Three hours to go.

He turned on the TV and lay back on the bed, ruminating on the possibility of doing a secret deal with Michael Lynch himself. Holland was the capital of the European criminal underworld, and the sale of a Caravaggio would earn him a lot more than twenty-five grand.

The best market for stolen art was Japan, thanks to their strange laws. Japanese law ruled that, once a collector could provide proof that a painting had been in his possession for a period of two years, the painting was legally his.

No, no, Peter finally decided; the Caravaggio was too hot now. Too much publicity. The job of getting it through the European channels to Japan would be too risky, especially with the Dutch police and Interpol on his tail. And, besides that, Caravaggio's *The Taking of Christ* was not really in accordance with Japanese taste. Their preference was for American and European *modern* art.

No, he would have to settle for the twenty-five thousand pounds and give the Caravaggio and the Irish thieves to the police.

*

At 7.45 p.m. Peter rang Reception and asked them to order a taxi to take him to South Great George's Street. Reception called him back a minute later, to say the taxi was on its way.

'Good,' Peter replied, and hung up. He returned to the mirror and checked his appearance one last time, smoothing a hand over his short-cut brown hair. His jacket was Armani and tan-coloured, his shirt yellow, and his trousers dark brown — all the autumn shades of a Rembrandt.

Finally he checked the charm of his smile in the mirror. Peter had always admired his own charisma, a necessary asset in the world of business.

He picked up his room-card and slipped it into his breast pocket. If the food at the Chinese restaurant wasn't good, he would console himself, upon his return to the hotel, by destroying room service with an order so big they would think he was a millionaire.

*

As soon as Peter stepped out of the elevator, Alec Duignan recognised him. They had met briefly in Amsterdam, and Peter had assured him that not only would he have no problem in finding a buyer for the painting, he would fence it himself for the usual commission.

Alec walked across the lobby and stopped Peter at the desk. 'Good to see you again, Peter,' he said pleasantly.

'Alec...' Peter looked surprised. 'Have you come to drive me to the restaurant? Shall I cancel my taxi?'

'I've already cancelled it,' Alec said.

He clasped Peter's elbow and led him away from the desk, lowering his voice. 'The plan has been changed. The boss wants to get the business done before he sits down to enjoy his meal in the restaurant. That's okay with you, isn't it?'

'Not really,' Peter said stonily. 'I have not eaten since I arrived today, and now I am very hungry. I would prefer to go straight to the restaurant.'

'Ah, sure, you'll be there in about an hour; the business won't take long.'

Alec tugged harder on Peter's elbow and led him towards the rear of the hotel. 'Come on, the boss is waiting for you in the bar.'

Again Peter showed his surprise. 'He is *here*, in the hotel?'

'Yeah.' Alec's grin was boyishly sociable. 'He thought it'd be good if we all had a few drinks in the bar before we go on to the Chinese.'

*

It was not the main bar, but the bar of the hotel's nightclub, which was fairly empty at the moment but would fill up later on. Michael and Tony Brady were sitting at a corner table in the shadows, away from the dance floor.

When Peter arrived at the table, Michael's greeting was very friendly. 'You don't mind, do you, Peter? Business before pleasure.'

Fucking Irish, never keep to the arrangements or timetable, Peter thought resentfully. But he smiled widely, showing his dentist-cleaned white teeth.

'No, of course not. But I hope it won't be too long before we get to the restaurant. I'm starving.'

'If you're that hungry, we can eat here as soon as we've finished talking business,' Michael suggested.

'No, no, I'll wait,' Peter said quickly. 'I've never liked English food — too bland. My favourite dishes are French or Oriental, perhaps a little Italian, but tonight we will all enjoy Chinese, ya?'

Michael looked at him silently.

Peter suddenly wondered if the Irishman was becoming suspicious because of his insistence upon the restaurant. If so, he would have to remedy the situation quickly. Tonight was not as important as tomorrow, the viewing of the painting. Only the capture of the gang and the Caravaggio together would secure his twenty-five grand.

'Oh, what the hell,' Peter said good-humouredly. 'We will stay here if you like. I am in Ireland, so I will be happy to eat Irish food. A good steak, perhaps? What does it matter, as long as we all have a good time and arrange our business satisfactorily?'

A waiter arrived at the table. Michael asked, 'What will you have to drink, Peter?'

'The drinks are on me,' Peter said. With a dramatic flourish, he turned to the waiter and ordered a bottle of champagne. He took out his room-card and showed it. 'Room 206. Put all the drinks on my bill, ya?'

As soon as the champagne was poured, Peter got down to business. He and Michael faced each other across the table. Peter leaned forward and lowered his voice.

'Here's the deal,' he said. 'I have a buyer. A Dutch Arab. He is prepared to pay five million Dutch guilders or two million English pounds for all of the Caravaggio paintings taken from the gallery. Or three million guilders or one million pounds for only *The Taking of Christ*.'

Michael said coolly, 'Only one Caravaggio is for sale. The big one.'

'But you have them all?'

'I have only one painting for sale,' Michael repeated noncommittally.

'Very well, the biggest and the best only,' Peter accepted. 'My buyer will be happy with that.' He gave Michael his charming smile. 'I told him you would not put all the paintings up for sale in one go. You are too clever for that.'

Michael accepted this flattery stone-faced. 'So do we have us a deal? The Caravaggio for one million pounds, right?'

'Right,' Peter agreed. 'But, of course, first I must be allowed to see the painting,' he added, 'to authenticate it.'

'Don't worry,' Michael said, 'I wouldn't expect your client to buy a pig in a poke. You'll get a chance to examine the painting tomorrow.'

'Fantastic!' Peter exclaimed. Then he waved cheerily to a waiter and gestured for him to bring more champagne.

*

An hour and three bottles of champagne later, Peter seemed to have forgotten all about the Chinese restaurant. He was slightly inebriated and clearly enjoying the Irish humour of his companions. Alec and Tony had given up after the first bottle of champagne and changed their drink to whiskey.

Only Michael was cold sober. He had raised his champagne glass to his mouth numerous times but had not drunk from it. Twice, while Peter's attention was distracted, Alec had quickly whipped up Michael's glass of champagne and knocked it back for him. Not even for a big-money deal would Michael break his no-alcohol rule, but he pretended to be almost as drunk as the others, laughing hilariously with Peter at every joke cracked.

The hotel's nightclub was packed now; it always was on Friday nights.

Peter emptied his glass and refilled it with champagne. He took a gulp, then leaned towards Michael.

'This fucking hotel,' he said drunkenly. 'The room they gave me is too small, not big enough. I'm going to ask — no — I'm going to *demand* to be moved to a suite.'

Alec laughed and slapped him on the shoulder. 'You do that, Peter. Demand your rights.'

'Ya.' Peter nodded. 'I'm a busy businessman, not a lazy tourist. I need room to move around.' He grinned slyly. 'I also need a woman. Do you know where to get me one?'

'Sure I do,' said Michael, standing up. 'But first I need to make a phone call. Won't be long.' He nodded towards a girl sitting at the bar. 'But you know what, Peter, I think that slapper's got her eye on you.'

'What's a slapper?' Peter asked innocently.

Alec and Tony laughed hilariously, then endeavoured to explain. Michael left them to it and slipped through the crowded bar, out to the lobby.

Some time earlier, while ordering more drinks, Peter had carelessly left his room-card on the table. Michael had deftly palmed it and slipped it into his pocket.

Now he walked across the lobby and took the elevator up to the second floor. Outside the door of Peter's room, he inserted the card-key in the lock and opened it, then switched on the light.

The room was not small at all, but spaciously pleasant and well furnished. He began to look around, opening drawers and searching through them. Nothing.

He opened the wardrobe and immediately saw, on the

floor at the back, a brown briefcase. He lifted it out and carried it over to the bed. If it was locked, he knew he could open it; but it wasn't locked. Two clicks of the catches and it was open.

Inside the briefcase he found what he was looking for: a list of contact numbers, including one for Commissioner Daly and others for Dutch police personnel.

He searched further, and his attention was caught by a small torch. He turned it on and off. Something about the torch wasn't right, but he couldn't work out what...

He opened it up and discovered a small transmitter and microphone inside.

Michael sat down on the bed, angry. So the tulipy Dutchman thought it was that easy to fuck the Irish, did he?

He carefully replaced the torch in the same place where he had found it, then put the briefcase back in the wardrobe, switched off the light, closed the door, and returned to the nightclub.

'Sorry, Peter, you're out of luck,' Michael said in a regretful voice, when he rejoined the table. 'The girl I rang for you — no answer from her phone.'

'That's okay.' Peter was in good form, his eyes on the girl at the bar. 'I like the look of that slapper.'

Chapter Nineteen

Following instructions, Peter telephoned Commissioner Daly at ten o'clock the following morning and explained why the meeting had not taken place in the Chinese restaurant. The arrangement had been changed by Michael Lynch at the last minute — all beyond Peter's control.

'I had to go along with them,' Peter said. 'I did not want to raise their suspicions.'

'Has he agreed to let you view the painting?' Daly asked.

'Ya, this afternoon. I will be collected at my hotel around noon. I am instructed to be ready.'

'Are you sure Lynch has no suspicions?'

'I thought so at first, but no, we can relax. Lynch is very keen for me to see the painting. He is eager to get the deal done as soon as possible.'

'Excellent!' Daly exclaimed. 'And you have the necessary equipment?'

Peter glanced at the small torch in his breast pocket. 'We can test it if you like.'

'Yes, do that.'

Peter put the phone aside and walked to the other side of the room. He lowered his mouth towards his breast pocket and said a few sentences.

Commissioner Daly heard every word clearly.

'Now listen,' Daly instructed, when Peter returned to the phone. 'On the journey, try and get the driver to tell you where you're going. That will make following you a damn sight easier. We can't follow too closely, under the normal surveillance procedure. This operation is too important to risk them spotting a tail. So keep talking conversationally to the driver, asking him things like "Where is this place?" and "Where are we now?" — like a tourist. But however you do it, try and keep us informed of where you are at every stage. Did Lynch give you any indication of whether the viewing would be outdoors or indoors?'

'No indication at all.' Peter hesitated. 'I was thinking that perhaps I should —'

'Don't think. Don't make any change to the plan. Just follow my orders. Good luck.'

Peter decided he did not like Commissioner Daly. But then, he disliked all policemen. He was working for them now solely to get some much-needed money.

He went into the bathroom and began to shave. He examined his face in the small mirror above the sink, and knew he was looking into the eyes of a defeated man who was still feeling upset by such an unexpected rejection the night before. Despite all his charming encouragement, and the champagne he had bought her, the slapper had refused to go to bed with him.

*

Commissioner Daly stepped out of his office and rubbed his hands in gleeful anticipation and premature satisfaction. The operation he had planned was going to be a great success.

Of course, Daly thought sourly, Noel Quigley was not
entirely convinced the plan would work. But then, Noel
Quigley had an aversion to giving credit to anyone but
himself. Such a tiring man.

Noel Quigley was sitting at his desk in the Operations
Room when Commissioner Daly walked in. The room
was a hive of activity. Garda officers were standing in
front of huge maps on the wall, marking where their cars
would stand ready; all the screens of the new computers
were on, the phones ringing, the whole place a buzz of
electronic efficiency.

It was all a bit scary to Daly, all this new computer
technology. But still, if it got the job done faster, why
complain?

*

'Whatever you do,' Michael had instructed Alec, 'do not
let Peter know where you are taking him. Right?'

'Right.'

Alec had a slight hangover. The champagne which
Peter had kept ordering the night before had tasted like
fizzy lemonade, and Alec had drunk too much of it,
followed by a good few whiskeys — although he knew it
wasn't the whiskey that had upset his head. Well, never
again. The millionaires could keep their frothy French
champagne; from now on, Alec was sticking to plain old
Irish or Scotch.

Alec reached the hotel fifteen minutes early. He went
inside and asked Reception to ring Peter and tell him his
taxi had arrived.

Ten minutes later, Alec took the elevator up to the
second floor and knocked on Peter's door.

Peter was still preening himself. He gave Alec a casual

smile. 'Come in and sit down for a few minutes.'

Alec followed him inside but didn't sit down, just wandered around the room jangling his car keys.

'How did it go with the slapper?' he asked.

Peter was adjusting his tie. 'She was like a tiger,' he said tiredly. 'Almost ripped the skin off my back. A crazy woman. I didn't like her very much, but I couldn't get rid of her. She left me alone about an hour ago.'

'Poor you,' Alec grinned. 'Last time a woman attacked me like that was never.'

Peter glanced at him, surprised. Alec was tall and dark and a very good-looking young man, with lots of sex appeal.

'No? No woman has ever attacked you sexually? Are you ... interested in girls?'

'Only my fiancée.' Alec leaned languidly against the wall and put a hand against his aching brow. 'And she's too soft to attack anyone. We've been together since we were kids.'

Peter pulled a face. 'Just the one? Are you not bored?'

'No.'

'I would find one woman very boring.'

'Not me. I'd prefer ten minutes with my Tina to a night with any slapper.' Alec swung his keys around a finger. 'Come on, are we going?'

'I'm ready.'

When they reached the car, Alec suddenly turned and looked at Peter curiously. 'Where's your equipment?'

'What equipment?'

'To examine the picture. Didn't you say, last night —'

'Oh, ya — I meant this.' Peter pointed to the small torch sticking up out of his breast pocket. 'It's all I need to authenticate the painting.' He grinned. 'A torch and my expert knowledge.'

'Fair enough,' Alec replied, then got behind the wheel
to do what he was expert at — driving cars.

As they drove out of the city, Alec remembered
Michael's instruction: *Whatever you do, don't let Peter know
where you are taking him.* He wondered about Michael's
reason, then shrugged; the boss was always very cautious.

Passing through Sandymount, Peter looked through
the window at the stretch of silver sea and asked, 'Where
are we now?'

'Not far from town.'

And that was when Peter started to talk much louder
than he needed to, and began to give Alec a severe
headache.

A few times Alec turned his head and frowned at
Peter, unable to understand why the Dutchman was
talking so loudly — they were sitting in a car, for God's
sake, not a noisy nightclub.

'And don't tell him a damn thing about anything,'
Michael had also warned. 'No matter how much he
questions you, act dumb and say nothing.'

That alone should have alerted Alec that something
wasn't right. Maybe it was the hangover that had caused
him to just nod without thinking about the *why* of it. Only
one thing was certain: Michael was treating the fence
with extreme caution.

But then, Michael treated everyone like that, Alec
realised.

'Do you like art generally?' Peter asked loudly. 'What
did you think of the painting? It is a beautiful Caravaggio,
is it not?'

Alec leaned forward to the dashboard and picked up a
strip of chewing-gum, unwrapping it expertly with one
hand and popping it into his mouth. He chewed silently
as Peter talked on through miles and miles of road.

'Of course, I realise it is the *money* which is your main interest in all this,' Peter said. 'The money you will get from the sale of the Caravaggio. Tell me about the robbery. Was it very difficult to pull off?'

When Alec just kept on chewing, Peter sighed resignedly and moved his mouth closer to the torch in his breast pocket. 'You obviously do not like to talk. You have no interest in conversation.'

Alec turned his head, offended. 'No, I love a good chat.'

'So why won't you talk to me?'

'I'm driving. I never talk when I'm driving.'

Peter pointed ahead and said loudly, 'So this must be the Dublin Mountains, ya?'

Alec nodded.

'Oh, it is good ... very beautiful. So these are *the Dublin Mountains*. Let us hope the weather remains fine. Especially if we have to view the painting outdoors... Tell me, Alec, will I be viewing the painting *outdoors*?'

Alec kept on chewing his gum.

*

The Hiace van was parked in a small clearing in the woods. Michael, Stevie and Tony stood waiting.

Alec drew the car to a halt a few yards away. Peter got out, full of effusive greetings for Michael. 'Now I can view?' he asked eagerly.

Michael nodded and opened the back door of the van. Stevie and Tony lifted out the painting.

'Where do you want it?' Michael asked.

'The Caravaggio?' Peter said loudly.

Michael looked at him archly, as if to say, 'What else?'

'Oh, upright somewhere.' Peter looked around. 'Perhaps if we lean it here against the van...'

Stevie and Tony positioned *The Taking of Christ* upright against the Hiace.

Peter took out his torch and flashed it onto the painting. 'Oh, ya,' he said loudly. 'It's so strange to be standing here, on a wooded mountaintop, looking at one of the great marvels of Renaissance art — Caravaggio's *The Taking of Christ*...'

As he knelt to make a closer inspection of the painting, a gun was suddenly jammed against the side of his head.

Peter's face went white. The other three men looked shocked. Michael's voice was icy quiet. 'What are you shouting for?'

'Oh, I — I'm sorry ... was I shouting?' Peter stuttered. 'I'm a little excited, perhaps. This is a very —'

Michael snatched the torch from him and pretended to examine it. He found the tiny microphone, and showed it to the others. The gun in his right hand was still jammed against the side of Peter's head.

Alec, Stevie and Tony looked at one another with furious dismay, although they didn't yet understand what Peter's game was.

'Right, Peter.' Michael spoke loudly into the microphone. 'Are you happy with your examination?'

He pressed the gun harder against Peter's skull and nodded for him to answer.

'Ya, ya, very happy.'

'Good.' Michael motioned to Stevie and Tony to pack up the painting and move quickly.

He grabbed Peter by the shoulder and pulled him to his feet, dragged him over to Alec's car, pushed him onto the back seat and slipped in beside him, still holding the gun on the Dutchman.

Michael spoke loudly into the torch. 'Right, lads, follow me. Back through Roundwood, okay?'

*

In the Operations Room at Garda Headquarters, Commissioner Daly was delighted. He checked the map and pointed.

'Roundwood. Got him!'

Daly spoke into his own microphone. 'Units 2, 3 and 6 — they're on their way to Roundwood. If you get there before him, I want a complete roadblock.'

*

Michael glanced through the back window. The Hiace, driven by Stevie, was closely following Alec's car down the mountain road.

Michael grinned as he kept his gun trained on the terrified Dutchman and spoke leisurely into the torch.

'Isn't the scenery around here just fantastic, Peter? Course, you've no mountains in Holland, have you?'

He nodded to Peter to reply.

'No, no, Holland is very flat.'

Michael nudged him to say more. Peter racked his brains... 'I love your country very much.'

'Same here, Peter. Ireland is a great place to live, d'you know that?' He called out to Alec. 'Are we near Roundwood yet?'

Alec played along, his voice loud. 'About half a mile, I'd say. Once we get off this road we're as good as there.'

'Fantastic.' Michael grinned at Peter. 'We might even stop for a pint in Roundwood, will we?'

*

Commissioner Daly exuded excitement as he spoke to his

units. Unmarked cars were hurtling towards Roundwood at a rate of knots.

'Are you in position, Units 2, 3 and 6? I want that roadblock rock-solid, do you hear me? Nothing, repeat, *nothing* is to get through.'

Noel Quigley was wearing headphones. He turned to Commissioner Daly, puzzled.

'Sir, the surveillance plane can't spot the target anywhere near Roundwood.'

'What?'

'The pilot, sir. He says he can't see any van.'

'What the hell is he talking about?'

'He says they're not in the area.'

'Well, they have to be,' Daly snapped. 'Maybe they haven't come out of the woods yet.'

*

Alec was happy to be back in familiar territory as he drove the car through a working-class suburb of Dublin.

Michael spoke into the torch's microphone. 'Here we go, Peter. There's Roundwood up ahead. It's supposed to be the highest village in Ireland, did you know that? I wouldn't mind living around here myself, I can tell you. A lovely spot.'

He nodded at Peter to speak.

Peter looked through the window at the teeming life on the city streets.

'It's ... very tranquil.'

*

'They're just coming into Roundwood now,' Commissioner Daly said to Noel Quigley.

Noel looked back at him, deadpan. 'Well, the surveillance plane still can't see them.'

'No?'

'No.'

Daly looked mystified. 'What's going on?'

He spoke to his units again, and couldn't believe at first what they were saying to him...

Then, finally, Daly did believe them. His eyes protruded like golf balls. 'Oh, fuck ... Lynch has done it again, made right fools of us... Oh, fuck! Oh, God forgive me for cursing — but fuck, fuck, *fuck*!'

He turned and glared venom at Noel Quigley. Now the upstart would be able to walk around with an I-told-you-so smirk on his arrogant face.

Noel was indeed smirking, knowing he would be empowered by Daly's cock-up.

*

Alec drove slowly past the main entrance of Garda Headquarters, then halted and reversed carefully to get close to the kerb.

In the back seat, Michael smiled ruefully at Peter. 'You know, this has all been a complete waste of Irish tax-payers' money.'

Peter stared back at him. His mouth was now gagged, his hands and feet were tightly tied, and the microphone was still sticking up from his breast pocket.

Michael leaned across him to open the door, then pushed him hard out of the car, leaving Peter dumped on the pavement outside Garda Headquarters.

*

Alec picked up speed and drove the car out to the warehouse. The Hiace van followed closely behind.

'Yeow!' Alec yelled, when they stopped inside the warehouse. 'That was just fucking amazing — what a buzz!'

Michael sat back in the car and sighed deeply. His adrenalin was rushing, the way it always did when he pulled a joke on the gardaí.

Tony yanked open the car door, his face angry. 'You knew all along, didn't you?'

Michael looked at him innocently. 'How do you mean?'

'Like, explain it to me. What did we go through all that for — if you knew Peter was a fake?'

'And a *bad* fake, at that!' Michael couldn't help chuckling. 'They're going to feel so stupid. Their snout dumped back on their doorstep. They're going to think there's no fucking way they can ever get the better of us.'

Tony looked dubious. 'Yeah, maybe. But I wouldn't try that one with Stevie right now. He's furious.'

'Stevie?' Michael shrugged. 'Fuck him, if he has no sense of humour.'

Chapter twenty

A thoughtful expression on his face, Detective Sergeant Noel Quigley sat in his office and contemplated the situation.

One thing he had learned long ago: if you let people get away with the small things, they will treat you like a fool and think they can get away with everything.

And that was just what Michael Lynch thought he could do with the police now. He should have been stopped at the beginning. Every time he'd been suspected of involvement in a crime, he should have been hauled in for hard questioning and tough treatment, and not allowed to get away with all his ridiculous alibis.

Quigley had spent days searching through Lynch's file, and he had noticed one important factor — two locations that Lynch regularly used for his alibis: the unemployment office, and police stations.

Well, not any more.

From now on, the gardaí would attack Michael Lynch so hard, he wouldn't know what had hit him. He would be given no room to manoeuvre, no time for crime, and no place for alibis.

Quigley stood up and walked out to the main office, where Detective Gerard Murphy was sitting at one of the desks leafing through a file.

'Whose file is that?'

Gerard looked up. 'Tony Brady's.'

'Give it to one of the others. I want you to cover Lynch with me.'

Gerard's face remained expressionless. 'Are we ready to go, then?'

'We will be on Monday morning,' Noel said. 'But before that, the main thing we have to do, and promptly, is get Michael Lynch taken off the government's payroll.'

'Eh?'

'The dole, Gerard. Get in touch with the relevant civil servants at the Department of Social Welfare and have Lynch's dole payments stopped.'

'Can we do that?'

'Of course we can — if the Department agrees that an investigation is needed into his present circumstances and therefore all payments must be suspended.'

Noel patted his pockets, looking for his lighter and cigarettes. 'And tell them to make sure it's a *long* investigation, Gerard. Three or four months at least. Then, once Lynch is without his dole allowance, he'll have to come up with a better excuse for where he's getting the money to pay his bills.'

*

Michael Lynch was fantasising about retiring from crime, giving it all up and going straight, maybe opening his own business or something. Breda was curled up on his lap, watching television.

Michael looked over at Christine and Lisa, sitting on the sofa. 'Listen, girls, I've been thinking ... do you think I should call it a day?'

'What?' Christine's eyes were fixed on the TV screen. 'Go up to bed, do you mean?'

'No, no ... I mean work.'

'In what way?'

'I mean, like, retire.'

Christine nodded. 'Yeah, sure.'

Lisa had to laugh. '*You*, retire? Sure, you couldn't stay off the mooch for a week, even.'

'No, the thing is, I'm not going to be able to do anything better than the last job. The Caravaggio. Anything else would just seem like Mickey-Mouse stuff, you know.'

Christine suddenly looked at him and realised what he was saying. 'But you'd drive us mad if you gave it up.'

'Yeah,' Lisa agreed. 'Hanging around under our feet day and night. No way, Michael.'

'I wouldn't, I swear,' he protested. 'Anyway, whenever you get fed up, yous can pass me over and back between the two of ye.'

Christine could see he was serious. 'Do you really want to? Give it all up?'

'Ah, yeah, I think so.' He looked fondly at his daughter, curled up in his arms. 'And you know what politicians say when they get fucked out — I want to spend more time with my family.'

*

Early on Monday morning, while Michael and Christine slept, two unmarked police cars drove up and parked outside the front of their house.

Detective Sergeant Noel Quigley and three detectives stepped out, looking very relaxed. All four lounged against their cars and lit up cigarettes.

Noel Quigley had abandoned all attempts to give up

smoking. It was now something he intended to do when the pressure was off, when Michael Lynch had been caught, convicted and put behind bars.

Noel smirked as he blew out a spiral of smoke. He was feeling very pleased with himself this morning. Headquarters had finally agreed to give him full control of the Michael Lynch operation, allowing him to handle the matter in his own way.

Noel had assured them of his eventual success.

His gaze ranged over the three detectives smoking with him. Michael Lynch didn't know these three, or the ones detailed at the back of the house. And Lynch would find these new guys harder to fool than Barry and Con and those other eejits Daly had used. This new team had been carefully selected — all younger, tougher and sharper than those used before. They were top men brought in from stations all over the country. The theft of the Caravaggio masterpiece from Ireland's National Gallery had upped the ante; only the best to catch Lynch from now on.

And catch Lynch they would. Quigley was certain of that.

*

Michael was still asleep. Christine pulled on her dressing-gown and went into the front bedroom to wake Tommy and Shane for school.

Seconds later she returned to the back bedroom and looked through the window, then rushed over to the bed and tried to wake her husband. 'Michael ... *Michael!* Take a look at what's happening outside.'

Michael moved as if a heavy hand was pressing his face into the pillow. 'What?'

'Just look. Front and back.'

He knew from her voice that something was wrong.

He sprang up, went to the window and peeked out: three detectives were perched on the wall at the back of the garden, drinking tea.

Michael looked at Christine. 'How did they get there?'

He hurried to the front of the house and into the boys' bedroom, where he looked out the window and saw Noel Quigley and three others lounging against their cars, smoking, as if they had nothing at all better to do.

Noel Quigley saw him at the window — and waved up to him.

Michael turned away. 'What the hell's going on?'

He went back to his own bedroom and Christine. 'D'you see what's happening out there?' he yelled. 'It's fucking illegal! Without any proof of a crime, or any charge of a crime, the gardaí have surrounded my home. That's deliberate intimidation and police harassment — and fucking *illegal*.'

'Are you saying the police are breaking the law?'

'Course they are! *Covert* surveillance of a suspect is allowed, but not this open fucking circus.'

*

Tony, Alec and Stevie arrived at the house later in the morning, each with two unmarked cars following him. Michael and Christine stared in disbelief as ten cars crowded for space outside their front garden.

'Jesus,' Stevie said as he entered. 'What's going on? The fuckers were parked outside my house even before I woke up.'

'Mine too,' Tony said.

Alec nodded. 'I did everything with my wheels to shift them, but they kept right on my tail all the way.'

'Right,' Michael decided. 'Let's see what their game is.'

Christine peeped out of the window. The detectives all gave her a wave.

Michael pulled up his hood and told the others to do the same. 'Come on, so. Let's see what they're up to. This is some new thing, but remember, whatever they do or say — ignore them. They don't exist.'

*

The detectives sprang alert when the front door opened and the gang walked out to their cars. They instantly started heckling, their voices loud and nasty.

'That him, yeah? Is that Lynch?'

'Yeah.'

'And that fuck is supposed to be a criminal master-mind? You must be joking. He's just a thick gobshite who got lucky, I'd say.'

'Well, he's fucked now. They're all fucked.'

Noel Quigley stood smirking.

Michael and the men managed to keep their cool, refusing even to acknowledge the detectives' presence.

As Michael tried to drive away, one of the unmarked cars pulled in front of him and blocked his departure. It was Quigley's car.

Gerard Murphy was sitting behind the wheel. He leaned out the window and shouted viciously.

'You can feel it, can't you, Lynch? Hey, Lynch, are you listening? You might as well give up now, because no matter what you do, we're going to be glued to your arse from now on.'

Michael ignored them; they did not exist.

Noel Quigley waved to him boastfully as their car pulled out to let him pass, then followed closely behind.

*

On Tuesday morning, Michael left his house and set off on his motorbike for his regular appointment at the dole office. It was an appointment he kept each week, without fail, and had kept for years.

His reason for doing this was not solely the money. More importantly, without his unemployment payments he would not be able to show any visible means of support, which would only give the police more ammunition against him, more evidence to accuse him of getting his money from crime.

In the queue at the unemployment office, when he reached the window, Michael was his usual polite self as he gave his name and smiled at the nervous clerk.

'Michael Lynch. And how are you today?'

The clerk had been waiting all morning for this with a feeling of dread. His hands were trembling as he silently passed over a slip of paper.

'What's this?'

'Your benefits have been ... er ... suspended.'

Michael gave him a cold stare. 'Try that one again?'

'It's the government. They've cut off your payments.'

The sudden silence around the dole office was stunning. Every person could feel the chill from Lynch, and waited tense and alert.

'Why have they cut off my dole? I don't have regular employment. I've been found guilty of no crime. So why the fuck?'

Noel Quigley and the other detectives standing at the main door were all smirking.

The clerk said quietly, 'I'm just following orders.'

Michael abruptly turned his head, a malevolent gleam in his dark eyes as he stared at Noel Quigley. For the first time it looked like he might break.

Noel certainly hoped so.

But instead he turned back to the clerk and said matter-of-factly, 'No one has to slavishly follow orders. Not if they're men. Didn't you know that, yeh stupid prick?'

The clerk indulged in a huge sigh of relief when Michael Lynch turned away; but a second later he turned back.

'Give me the docket to sign anyway.'

The clerk whispered, 'What?'

'Give me the docket to sign. Even though my payments have been suspended for no good or valid or legal reason, I still want to sign and confirm that I am unemployed.'

When he left the office he was followed by his two smirking chaperones, who gibed at him spitefully and incessantly, but he gave no response. They did not exist.

They were not going to beat him. Michael was determined about that. They had shown their hand, revealed their plan, and so he thwarted it.

Every Tuesday he continued to arrive at the dole office, as usual, and sign the docket to confirm that he was still unemployed.

Chapter twenty-One

At the end of four weeks, everyone was tired of the cat-and-mouse chase, except the detectives.

Every day, everywhere Michael and the others went, detectives followed and could not be shaken off.

Michael finally decided to take Noel Quigley and his sarcastic colleague for a long drive up to the Wicklow Mountains.

As soon as he reached the deserted country roads, the reaction of the driver behind astonished him; he came in close and almost hit Michael's bumper.

He accelerated, but the police car did the same and rammed him harder this time, as if trying to knock him off the road.

Okay, if it was a bit of fun they wanted... He pressed the accelerator to the floor, screaming forward, the speedometer rising higher and higher until it was touching ninety. He almost went into a tailspin as he turned a corner, mounting the grass on the opposite side of the road, but he managed to keep the car steady and going forward.

He glanced back. No sign of the unmarked car, or any car; he had lost them.

His foot eased back on the pedal until his speed

slowed to forty, and for the first time in weeks he felt free. No one tailing him, no one sitting outside his front and back doors, no one walking close to his shoulder at every step.

He took a deep, relaxing breath and gazed at the green wilderness around him, and for the first time he appreciated how peaceful it would be to live in the country, away from people, away from pressure. Maybe he would buy a house in the country one day, a retreat for himself and the two families.

A rueful smile passed over his face as he thought of Christine and Lisa being asked to leave Dublin and live in the country; they would hate it. They loved the shops and the cinemas and the restaurants, and all the hustle and bustle of the city. A quiet, isolated life was not for them. Ah, well...

A sound made him turn his head and look back, just as the unmarked police car careered out of a side lane and sped towards him.

They were back on his tail.

He kept his speed steady at forty, and the car behind did the same. He put a Van Morrison tape in the stereo and tried to ignore them, listening to the music as he drove for miles and miles through Wicklow.

On a remote mountain road, he noticed his fuel gauge reading almost empty and stopped. If his tank was near empty, then so must theirs be. Smiling slightly, he got out of the car and walked to the boot, took out the five-gallon drum and refuelled.

'Fuck you, Lynch,' Noel Quigley laughed, holding up his own five-gallon drum. 'That's an old gag of yours!'

Michael got back in the car, still refusing to acknowledge their presence. But as he drove away he took a deep breath and blew out his lips. The old gags would have to be replaced with new ones.

*

Three days later, in Winetavern Street, in the heart of the city, Michael's car, Alec's car, Stevie's car and Tony's car deliberately swerved and blocked the street.

Lisa and the other wives and girlfriends were passengers.

Each car was pursued by two unmarked police cars, causing a further eight cars to be caught in the roadblock.

Michael and the other men quickly jumped out of their cars and darted into an alleyway, leaving chaos behind as detectives leaped out of their cars to give chase. Other vehicles, blocked behind the empty police cars, blared their horns furiously.

Lisa got out when Noel Quigley tried to clamber over her car and get past her. She looked around her and spoke loudly to no one in particular:

'Could somebody please call the guards? To sort out this mess. They're never around when you need them.'

'His time is up, Lisa!' Quigley told her. 'It's gone way past a joke, and I think you know it.'

She watched Quigley tear down the alley like a dog chasing a cat.

*

On Winetavern Street Bridge, crossing over to the other quay, the rest of the gang voiced their frustration to Michael, especially when they saw the detectives running like crazy to catch up with them.

'How long can they keep this up?' Tony asked. 'How many have they got doing this?'

'There must be a hundred,' said Stevie. 'And I don't know any of them. All this is doing my head in.'

'Don't let it,' Michael said. 'Keep smiling at them.' He

turned his head and grinned at the pursuing detectives.

'Bastard!' one of them shouted.

Stevie said, 'I've had a contact about the painting, Michael.'

'Yeah?'

'An offer. From the IRA.'

Michael kept walking. Stevie looked for some visible reaction from him, but there was none.

'A straightforward, no-bullshit offer,' Stevie continued. 'One hundred grand. Not great, I know, but better than having the thing just rot away.'

When Michael gave no answer, Stevie continued, 'And Jerome Higgins said to tell you that if you did the deal, then it would be all right about Billy.'

Michael shot him a dark look. 'Sorry?'

'Like ... you could let Billy come back to Dublin. There'd be no hassle.'

Michael paused. 'You talked to Jerome Higgins about Billy?'

'Look, if we do this,' Stevie said, 'those fuckers, the gardaí, they'll go after the IRA and leave us alone.'

Alec found the courage to speak up. 'Anyway, it's not our thing, Michael. You know — art stuff. We're not in that league.'

It was the wrong thing to say. Stevie and Tony glared at Alec, knowing he had blown it.

'See all these gardaí?' Michael said angrily. 'Just look what we've done to them. We've *dragged* them down to our level. *They're* the ones acting like criminals now. They don't know any other way to get to us. And me — I'm their worst fucking nightmare. And you're telling me we should give up the Caravaggio — the thing we'll be remembered for — and hand it over to Jerome Higgins, of all people? You think he'll give you a hundred grand?'

Stevie was adamant. 'Yeah, I do.'

'Like fuck he will! Can't you see what he's at? It's not about the Caravaggio; he doesn't really want that. It's about splitting us, dividing us. He wants to be his own crime boss, and he wants you experts on his payroll.'

Stevie wasn't prepared to listen. He said, 'All I know is that we're robbers, Michael. We rob for a living. And I'm not making a living any more.'

Michael fell silent, still walking.

Tony finally spoke. 'Will you at least think about it, Michael? What we've been saying?'

Michael glanced at him. 'You too, hah?'

Tony's look was full of apology. 'Yeah. That painting may be a masterpiece, but to us it's been nothing but a fucking jinx. Let's take the IRA's cash and be done with it.'

Michael shrugged. 'Tell Higgins I'll let him know.'

'I'll be letting him know, too,' Stevie said gravely. 'And I hope we'll be telling him the same thing.'

They had reached the end of the bridge. Michael glanced behind. The detectives were following in a group. 'Everyone split onto different paths,' he said.

The gang fanned out in four separate directions. Michael was glad to be walking on his own. He needed to think.

Noel Quigley caught up and doggedly followed him.

Michael ignored him. He did not exist.

But Noel Quigley kept close to his shoulder every step of the way, even while Michael picked his children up from school.

Chapter twenty-two

'**M**ichael Lynch. And how are you today?'

The clerk behind the counter in the unemployment office was used to this performance. Michael Lynch still turned up every week to sign and confirm that he was unemployed, even though he received no benefits.

But this week was different. This week the clerk didn't have a docket for Michael Lynch to sign.

'Mr Lynch,' he said gravely, 'the Department has completed its investigations, and it has been decided that you are no longer entitled to any benefits. So there's no use in you signing anything.'

Michael stared at him. 'Are you trying that on me again? I'm unemployed, so I'm entitled to register as unemployed. Give me the docket to sign.'

'I can't. The decision is final. You are permanently to lose all welfare benefits. So there's no point in you even coming here any more.'

'No point in even coming to the dole office?' Michael paraphrased. His masculinity was insulted, his pride reduced to shreds, yet all he did was smile at the clerk as if it really didn't matter that much.

But underneath his smile, he was seething.

'I'm sorry, Mr Lynch, I'm just following orders.'

Michael kept on smiling. 'Still following orders? Ah, you're just too good a man for your own interest.'

The clerk didn't know if he was being complimented or disparaged, but he didn't care. He was just very glad to see the back of Michael Lynch as he left the line and walked away.

*

When Michael reached the door, Noel Quigley and Gerard Murphy were waiting for him, smirking in their usual way. *Like two ugly chipmunks*, Michael thought. They followed him outside, followed him to his car, then drove behind him all the way home.

When he entered the house, Christine and Lisa were in the kitchen having a natter. He burst in on them, in a vile temper.

'Girls, have ye a minute?'

Lisa stared at him. 'What's up with you?'

'Nothing. It's just these gardaí getting on my nerves... I want to go on the mooch tonight.'

Lisa gave Christine an I-told-you-so smile. 'So much for your retirement,' she said.

Michael snapped, 'Are you going to fucking help me or not?'

'Yeah,' Lisa snapped back. 'Keep your hair on.'

Michael tried to control himself. 'You don't understand. I can't take much more of this without fighting back. I'm being smothered everywhere I go, suffocated in my own home — even now the bastards are parked outside, watching every move we make. I've got to get out on my own tonight, I've got to go on the mooch, but I need you two to help me get past the detectives, yeah?'

Christine crossed to him and slipped her arms around his waist. 'Sure, we'll help you, love. Won't we, Lisa?'

Lisa was already regretting her sarcasm. She smiled softly at Michael. 'Course we will, Michael. You know you can always rely on us.'

He nodded. 'Thanks. But first I've got to make a few phone calls.'

He had no intention of going on the mooch, but he didn't want the women to know that. They wouldn't understand his rage. They hadn't a fucking clue about how men felt.

He left the kitchen and headed for the corner room, his brain whirring. He was down on his luck now, cornered and trapped, but he was going to fight back. One by one, he was going to deal with all his enemies, including that condescending little prick at the dole office.

Inside the corner room he made two phone calls. Three hours later, at 6.30 p.m., he received a return call giving him the information he needed.

'Are you sure, now? You waited and followed ... and that's definitely the right address?'

*

When Christine and Lisa drove into the city that night, two detectives in an unmarked car followed them.

They were having a girls' night out together, going to see a film. Christine parked in the underground car park near the cinema. The two detectives drew up beside them and got out of their car also. They leaned against their car and grinned and said a few words of friendly banter, but from Christine and Lisa there were no smiles, no acknowledgement; it was as if the detectives didn't exist.

They were halfway across the car park, with the two

detectives close behind, when Christine suddenly stopped walking and said loudly to Lisa, 'Oh, wait now — I'd better take the car radio out and put it in the boot. They'd rob anything these days.'

She ran back to the car, took out the radio and went round to the boot. As soon as she opened it, Michael slid out.

'Better to be safe than sorry,' Christine called to Lisa, putting the radio inside and slamming the boot shut.

Michael remained crouched down behind the car, watching Christine run back to Lisa, then the sisters chattering on as they walked out of the car park, with the two detectives following them out to the street.

It's really disgusting, Michael thought. *Two innocent women unable to go to the pictures without two baboons from the gardaí following and watching them all the way. Sure, the KGB in Russia could never have been any worse.*

Michael left the car park and turned right into a side-street. Headlamps flashed on, and a battered old blue Ford Cortina drove up to meet him. Tom Rooney was behind the wheel.

'Jesus,' Michael said, when Tom got out of the car, 'where did you get this old thing?'

'It was the best I could do at such short notice,' Tom explained. 'You said you wanted something old that you could dump after, and I saw this parked outside a house on my way back from Kimmage. It seemed just perfect. Just sitting there waiting for me. No one saw me nip in and drive it away. But if you want to dump it back outside the same house after, I'll tell you where: it's the house with the blue door, next to —'

'It doesn't matter a wank where,' Michael cut him short. 'Just give me the picklock and let me get going.'

Tom handed over the picklock, designed to fit any lock, its bit carefully hollowed.

'She's got a nice big boot,' Tom said. 'Nice and roomy, you know. Solid, too. I used to have a Cortina meself once, did I ever tell you? She needed a bit of a wash when I bought her, but she cleaned up lovely. As good as a Rolls Royce, she was, but then —'

Michael heard no more as he closed the car door and started up the engine.

'Good luck!' Tom Rooney shouted through the glass.

Michael suddenly paused and rolled down the window. 'Listen, Tom,' he said appreciatively, 'you did your best for me, and you done good. I won't forget that.'

'Ah, sure,' Tom shrugged, 'that's what pals are for.'

*

It was 8.30 p.m. when Michael found the right house on the Kimmage Road. It was a main road, with intermittent cars going up and down, but the evening rush hour was long over and the night traffic was light.

The road was dark save for the yellow streetlamps, and fortunately the house was not directly under one of them. Even if it had been, Michael didn't think that would have stopped him; his rage was too great.

He got out of the car and looked up and down the street. Nobody about, but nearly all the downstairs windows of the houses were aglow with light, the curtains drawn, everyone settled in for a night in front of the TV.

He walked up to the front door and rang the bell. The top half of the door was frosted glass. The hall light was on. He couldn't have asked for better conditions.

As he waited for his ring to be answered, he noticed that the front of the house was very neat and tidy, with little terracotta flowerboxes on the ledges of the bay window.

He was about to ring the bell again when he heard a

sound from inside, someone coming down the hall. Through the frosted glass he could see the height and shape of the approaching figure, and he knew instantly that it was his man. He quickly pulled on his balaclava.

When the door opened, the clerk from the unemployment office found his arm grabbed and an automatic pistol jammed into his neck.

'*Jesus* — wha —'

'Shut the fuck up. You're going for a little drive.'

The clerk, stunned, cried out stupidly in his fright, 'A drive? With you?'

'No, with Sinéad O'Connor. Who the fuck do you think?'

The clerk was overweight, and he almost stumbled when Michael dragged him towards the car. 'Make another sound and I'll put a bullet straight between your eyes. A bullet that explodes and makes a hole the size of a plate. You want that?'

The clerk dumbly shook his head, then almost screamed again when he saw he was going into the boot of the car.

'I have asthma,' he gasped.

'Get your arse in!' Michael hissed, pushing the clerk down and inside until he was lying in a crouched position. Then he slammed the boot shut.

He glanced back at the house. The door was still open, but no one else had come to see who was at the door; such was the magnetic grip of the TV. Or maybe the clerk lived alone. Who the hell cared?

Seconds later he was behind the wheel, driving away from the Kimmage Road.

*

When the car finally stopped and the boot was opened, the clerk took a huge, gulping breath of air into his lungs.

He could smell the sea, but when he was pulled to his feet, all he could see in the dark night was the outline of a hedgerow, broken here and there. There was grass beneath his feet. He knew he was in some deserted wilderness, somewhere near the sea, but he hadn't a clue just where.

The gun was pressed to his neck again and he was dragged towards the bushes. This was some awful mistake.

'Listen,' he said in a tremulous voice to his abductor, 'will you at least give me some explanation of what this is about? You must have the wrong man.'

'No mistake, you're the man. And you're going to be taught a lesson.'

The clerk was pulled past the hedge, down a grassy bank, and positioned between two railway lines. He let out a gasp of horror. These were the lines that the DART trains sped up and down.

A blindfold was suddenly wrapped around his eyes.

'Before we start,' Michael said sarcastically, 'I'd just like you to know, I'm only following orders.'

He stepped back onto the grass. 'I wouldn't move if I were you,' he said. 'The trains won't hit you if you don't move.'

'Oh, Jesus...' The clerk was sweating. He could feel himself becoming a little sick and disorientated. In the distance, he could hear a DART approaching. He whimpered in terror.

'Don't move,' Michael said. 'Trust me.'

As the roar of the DART drew nearer, the clerk began a bubbling cry of fright, but his body stood rigid.

The DART flew past him, only inches away.

'You see,' Michael said, 'I told you you'd be safe if you didn't move. But, of course, they come in the other direction too. I don't know if you'll be safe from those. I suppose you will if you don't move.'

The clerk screamed out in his terror, 'Why are you doing this to me? Why? For God's sake, why?'

'To teach you something. Did you ever stand in a dole queue? Did you ever have to do that? Well, now you know what it's like. Waiting your turn. At someone else's mercy. Like a beggar. No respect. Powerless. No power at all. Have you any idea what it's like for men who, week after week, have to stand in the misery of the dole queue? No, of course you fucking don't.'

Another DART was approaching, on the other line.

The clerk screamed, 'Please, please tell me — am I all right? *Please!*'

'I told you to trust me. Just keep your nerve and don't move.'

The clerk screamed hysterically as the DART flew by, so close. In the aftermath of silence he stumbled forward to escape the tracks, crying with relief when he felt the grass bank beneath his feet.

'Right, I think you've learned something tonight,' Michael said coldly. 'So you can go home now. But you'll have to find your own way.'

Seconds, minutes, an eternity later, when he heard the car driving away, the clerk pulled the blindfold from his eyes and looked around him in the darkness. He could still smell the sea, and he thought he must be near Sandymount or Blackrock.

Then everything went fuzzy and he stumbled over to the hedge, holding on to its prickly branches as he lowered his head and was violently sick.

*

Christine and Lisa returned to the underground car park full of chat about the film. The two detectives followed behind, listening to every word.

'Wait'll I get the radio out,' Christine said.

She casually walked to the back of the car, opened the boot and retrieved the radio. She winked at Michael as he slid inside again, but he avoided her eye. She slammed the boot shut and grinned at Lisa as she opened the driver's door.

'The radio's safe and sound,' she said.

*

When Michael awoke the next morning, he was surprised to see that it was almost twelve. He'd had another bad night of tossing and turning, finally drifting off around dawn. His conscience had started bothering him, preventing him from sleeping. It was odd and unexpected that he felt no gratification after taking his revenge on the clerk. The truth was that, now he had done it, he felt bad.

It was a new feeling. After all, he had used beatings and threats in the past; but that had always been with other gangsters, men who knew the game and the rules and the consequences, not some poor little prick of a clerk from the mainstream.

Forget it; it was done and couldn't be undone. But he still felt bad.

When he walked into the kitchen, Christine was sitting at the table, drinking a cup of tea and reading a newspaper spread out on the table. She looked up and stared at him coldly, then looked away.

The newspaper carried a headline about the abduction and torture of a Social Welfare official.

She knew Michael had done it.

'I'm sorry, Christine.'

She stood up and faced him. 'You used Lisa and me.

You shouldn'ta done that. Not for what you did.'

'I know, I know... But when he told me they were cutting off my dole permanently, I just thought — I thought, like — this is fucking *it*. They're not going to do these things to me. They're not going to treat me like shit. And — well, I lost my head.'

'Can't you see where it's all heading, Michael?'

'I see now what they're trying to do.'

'It's all heading only the one way. You in prison. And it'll be twenty years. More, maybe. And me and Lisa and the kids will be left —'

'No, that's not going to happen —'

They both turned as a voice boomed into the house from outside. Noel Quigley, speaking through a megaphone.

'Hey, Lynch! This is Noel Quigley. Big mistake last night — or do you even know that? What was that supposed to be? Funny? Was that your idea of a joke? You're losing it, Lynch ... losing it fast.'

'You see,' Christine said, 'you said you were going to give it all up. And I believed you.'

'As long as you live, we'll be here, watching you. Do you get it? No escape.'

Christine swung round and ran to open the front door, shouting at Noel Quigley and the others. 'Stop it! Stop it! Leave us alone!'

She slammed the door so hard it nearly bounced off its hinges.

Standing in the hall, Michael looked furious. 'What're you doing? You know the last thing you should do is let them see they're getting to us.'

'Fuck off, Michael.'

She walked past him and sat on the bottom step of the stairs. She was upset, very upset.

Michael drew a deep breath and then sat down on the step beside her. 'I promise you, Christine, no matter what, they'll never put me away.'

'They're out to get you, Michael. What can you do about it?'

'I'll tell you what I can do. I can... I don't know.'

Christine was surprised at this admission.

He looked at her honestly. Who else in the world could he tell the truth to? Who else would understand? Only Christine.

'I'm afraid... Okay, I'm afraid you might be right. It's never happened to me before, but I'm not sure now. Will they wear me down, bit by bit, until... Because they won't get the better of me any other way. I won't let them. Never. I mean, if that happens ... then it was all worth nothing.'

Christine looked thoughtful. 'So what are we going to do?'

'Right now, I don't know.'

'What about the painting? The Caravaggio. If you got some money —'

'Sure, that was never about the money. That was all about the challenge and skill of thinking out a way to pull it off successfully. And I did that.' He smiled. 'No money yet, but we got a few great laughs out of it. Especially with Peter the tulipy Dutchman.' He smiled again at the memory.

Christine had always loved that smile.

She put her arms around him and kissed him. 'Do you know what you are? You're irrepressible, you're inimitable...'

Michael grinned. 'That good, yeah?'

'Well, you wouldn't be everyone's cup of tea. But you suit me.' She kissed him again, fuller and longer this time.

He felt forgiven. He felt her body relax against him.

She rested her head on his shoulder and he rubbed his face over her hair. 'Do you want to go upstairs?' he asked quietly.

She tilted her head and smiled at him, shook her head. 'No, I'd rather wait until tonight. You know I always go to sleep afterwards, and the kids will be home soon.'

'Ah, well,' he sighed. Then a sudden idea for a bit of fun came to him.

'Listen,' he said with a grin, 'why don't we let those fascists outside know what we think of them?'

He whispered seductively into her ear, and as she realised what he was suggesting, she burst out laughing.

'Yeah, why don't we,' she agreed mischievously. 'But you start it.'

'Okay, here we go.' Michael took in a deep breath, then let out the groan of a man in hot passion, oblivious to the world outside. A few seconds later Christine joined in...

Outside, Noel Quigley and the other detectives listened in silent shock to the spiralling moans and groans of spirited lovemaking coming from the house.

Noel looked at the others in disbelief.

After all he had said through his megaphone, after all he had warned and threatened — Lynch didn't give a fuck about it.

Chapter twenty-three

Later that afternoon the phone rang. Michael picked it up. It was Stevie Brady.

Stevie said simply, 'How're yeh?'

'Fine.'

'Are the gardaí still outside your door?'

'All the time.'

'Yeah, I know,' said Stevie. 'They're outside mine every fucking day and night too, and it's doing my head in.'

'Don't let them get to you. Keep smiling.'

'Easy for you to say. So what's going on, Michael?'

'How d'you mean?'

'About the Caravaggio. We didn't rob it just to look at it, you know. It was supposed to make us rich.'

'Yeah, I know... I'm trying to find a way to unload it. Maybe the fence in Manchester can do something.'

'Ah, bollix. We don't even know for sure that him and Tom Rooney didn't pull a scam on us with the gold. Funny there's never been a word about a door full of gold in the newspapers or anything.'

'Because it's never been found. All bets are on it being at the bottom of the River Severn.'

'You believe that?'

'Don't you?'

Stevie hesitated. 'I don't know... But listen, Michael, we've still got the painting. How's about we meet up tonight in a pub and discuss it? Like, get down to some *very serious* talk about it. I mean, you don't own it. We all do. We all robbed it. And the guards won't be able to get too close to us in a pub. They'll park outside like always.'

Michael was silent for a moment. He knew Stevie was getting edgy and impatient for a pay-off on the painting. And impatience always led to mistakes.

Stevie continued, 'The Yellow House pub. I'll meet you there at nine o'clock.'

*

It was dark when Michael approached the Yellow House pub. He looked at his watch; 8.40. He was twenty minutes early.

He had turned off the main road and down a side-street, ready to turn into the car park, when another car blocked his path, coming out. He reversed slightly to let the car pass. When it did, the driver drew alongside him and rolled down his window.

To his surprise, Michael saw that it was Jerome Higgins. His slimy grin was arrogant, full of triumph.

'So, Michael,' he said, 'are you ready now to do business?'

Michael kept his face impassive. 'What kind of business?'

'The Caravaggio.'

Michael glanced at his rear-view mirror and saw Quigley's unmarked car parked a few yards back on the street, but the windows were up. They probably thought Higgins was just some driver asking the way to some-where.

'The Caravaggio,' Michael said. 'What's that got to do with you?'

'I can give you a good price for it.'

'Ah, can you?' Michael's smile was full of relief. 'Well, you know, Jerome,' he said sincerely, 'the last time we met, I know I told you to fuck off, so you'll probably be very surprised now when I tell you ... to fuck off again.'

Higgins's face took on the dirtiest look Michael had ever seen.

'You'll be sorry, Lynch,' he warned. Then he shot forward and drove away from the car park.

Michael sat at the wheel, his brain whirring. *Why was Higgins here tonight? This particular pub? He must have known I was coming here and wanted to meet me — bump into me accidentally, to make his offer for the Caravaggio.*

But no, Michael suddenly realised; that couldn't be it. Because he wasn't due at the pub until nine, and Higgins had been leaving the car park twenty minutes before that.

He looked around the car park and saw that Stevie's car was already there, parked in the far corner... And then it all became clear. Higgins had come to the pub tonight to meet *Stevie*.

Higgins had got to Stevie and was dealing with him under the table. He had probably instructed Stevie on every word to say. And that was why the slime-bag had been slipping away before Michael arrived.

Michael sighed at the irony of it: the early bird really *does* catch the worm.

He reversed the car back onto the street. Stevie could go fuck himself. And he could do whatever deal he wanted with Higgins, because Michael Lynch still held the ace.

He smiled to himself as he thought of Caravaggio's original masterpiece hanging on the wall of the refectory in the Jesuit house. No one knew it was there, only him.

So if Stevie intended to go behind his back and sell the

painting to Jerome Higgins, then let him. All Higgins would get was a fake, a replica worth nothing.

And Michael Lynch would *still* hold the ace. He had never been a fool, and Stevie should have remembered that.

As he pulled out of the side-street, waiting his turn to pull onto the main road, he glanced back at the front entrance of the Yellow House and saw Tony Brady strolling towards it.

So Tony hadn't been in on the meeting with Higgins.

But he was surprised to see that the two detectives following Tony walked straight into the pub behind him.

Michael thought about that as he drove on. It seemed that even pubs weren't safe meeting-places any more.

*

When his shift was finished that night, Noel Quigley didn't go home. He had seen the driver in the other car talking to Lynch, and he thought he recognised him. But from where?

Back in his office, he sat at his desk and operated his desktop computer, which held all his personal notes and dossiers. He keyed in his own secret code, then spent over an hour looking at video images on the screen.

But no, nothing.

Whoever he was, he either wasn't a criminal or had never been convicted. So why had Quigley thought he recognised him?

And then it clicked: he looked a lot like Lynch, that was why. The same dark colouring, same structure of the head and face.

Quigley switched off his computer and stood up. But there was no chance that he would leave it at that. As a last shot, he went into the outer office, to the main computer, to check through the list of men who were suspected of being party to a crime but had never been caught or charged.

Two hours later, he finally found his man — yeah, it was him all right. On the surveillance photograph supplied he looked a real ringer for Michael Lynch, but his name was Jerome Higgins.

Quigley's eyes scanned down the short biog, and what he read made him rock back in his chair.

'I — R — fucking — A!'

Quigley could scarcely believe it. He had thought he knew everything about Michael Lynch, but he hadn't known this. Hadn't even suspected it. So since when had Michael Lynch taken up dealings with the IRA?

Chapter twenty-four

Finbar Sheridan was a man very content with life. On the two occasions that Michael Lynch had been in prison, Finbar had gone inside with him. On the first occasion they had tried to rob a bank and failed. On the second occasion they had robbed the same bank and succeeded, but had later been identified and convicted.

Ah, but that had been in their youth. After his second period in prison, Finbar had gone stráight.

Crime had just been a pastime of his juvenile years, Finbar often told his wife, never mentioning that he had been twenty-two at the time.

Uneducated as he was, Finbar had tried many menial jobs in his bid to go straight, but he was always fired because of one incurable handicap — he simply hated everyone, and suspected everyone of trying to do him down.

It was something that had been bred into him since he was a small child. His father had absconded and his mother had later abandoned him to be brought up by his grandfather, a grumpy and impoverished old man who had endured a hard life and truly hated the world.

'Life is miserable for most people,' his grandfather would say. 'We're put on this earth to suffer. Only the lucky die young.'

Finbar had supped these sayings with his porridge throughout his childhood years, and they had affected his psyche and his view of life.

'Most people pretend they're all right, and sometimes they even pretend they're happy, but they're just marking time,' his grandfather would say. 'Waiting for the last day or night to come. No one really likes this life. The only reason they keep sucking air in and out of their lungs is because they don't know how not to. Only the lucky die young.'

And after all his years of trying to go straight, it was finally the influence of his grandfather that guided Finbar to a job he loved.

He became an undertaker. He had finally found his place in the world, helping as many people as he could into the next world. He was their attentive chaperone to the grave, and he only wished his grandfather had lived long enough to see the good work he was doing.

He had started as an apprentice, diligently developing his skill, but now he owned his own establishment. And, ah, it was grand. A place to be proud of.

At the front was his funeral parlour — a reception room for mourners, with nice seats and fresh flowers on every surface. On the other side of the doorway was a room for storing the coffins. At the back was the large soundproofed embalming room containing all his chemicals.

But his favourite room of all was the little pantry where he kept his kettle and cakes, and he often sat down in there to read a newspaper and have a smoke. And it was during these times, reading the newspapers, that Finbar kept up to date on all of Michael Lynch's escapades.

Not that he needed to read the papers to know. Michael Lynch was a man who never forgot his friends.

Michael popped in to see Finbar now and again, and occasionally phoned him. It was Michael who had robbed a building society to get Finbar the money to open his own business. A true friend.

A few times, over the years, the two of them had met for a drink and a snack and a yack. And it had always been great craic, a great laugh, reminding Finbar of the years when they had run wild together, not giving a toss about anyone. Even in jail Michael had been great fun, always pulling off jokes; and no matter what the screws did to him in return, Michael Lynch had just kept on smiling.

Finbar was sitting in his little pantry, smoking a Silk Cut and reading the newspaper. There was an article in it about Michael Lynch, saying he was the biggest drug dealer in Dublin. It was reading it that had brought Michael into his mind.

Finbar shook the paper in disgust and turned the page. Michael Lynch had always been against drugs. That article was all a lie.

*

Three days later, Michael Lynch called in to the funeral parlour.

Finbar was in the front reception, having just taken a booking from a mourner. The room was empty now, the scent of flowers overpowering.

Finbar's head was still bowed in respect for the grief of the mourner. He always lowered his head and spoke in a soft voice to his clients. It snapped up when he saw Michael, and a delighted grin moved over his features.

'Ah, Michael, how're yeh? Long time no see.'

Michael couldn't help thinking that Finbar looked

terrible these days. He knew how much Fin loved his job — lived it, breathed it, worked all the hours necessary without a word of complaint — but even his face had become as pale as all his corpses.

'Are you feeling okay?' Michael asked with concern.

Finbar shrugged. 'I'm no longer a kid. Sometimes I wake up tired.'

Michael knew the feeling. He said, 'Fin, I need a favour.'

Finbar nodded. 'Anything.'

Michael glanced at his watch. 'In about fifteen minutes, a friend is coming to meet me in here. Is that okay?'

'Sure, certainly, of course. You know you don't even have to ask.'

'Thanks. I need to speak to him seriously and in private. Is it all right to use the storeroom?'

'Definitely, absolutely.' Finbar nodded. 'Come on and I'll take you over.'

The undertaker led the way across the hall into the storeroom, which was full of coffins made of all kinds of beautiful and gleaming wood.

'You'll be nice and private in here,' Finbar said. Then something outside the window caught his attention. 'What's all that about?'

He moved over to the window and peered over the net curtain that covered the lower half. There were about six men standing around outside, and two of them had their faces pressed right up to the glass, peering back at him.

Finbar jumped back and turned to Michael. 'Jesus, who're that lot?'

'My police escort, in plain clothes. They've increased their number from four to six. They follow me everywhere, like fucking shadows. They're driving me crazy, Fin. That's why I decided to meet Tony in here. This is not exactly a place they can barge into.'

'Just let them try,' Finbar replied murderously. 'I'd have them all embalmed before they could hand over a warrant. But now listen — forget about them; will I go into the back and make us a sup a tea?'

Michael smiled. That was Finbar's answer to everything: a sup a tea. 'All right, go on,' he said, 'but not too strong. The last mug of tea you made me nearly put me away.'

Finbar chuckled. 'Kept you going, more like.' His eyes were back on the window. The detectives were no longer peering in, but their voices could be heard talking to one another.

'Wait'll I get rid of this lot,' Finbar said furiously. 'I'll not tolerate anyone talking loud outside my funeral parlour, not even the fucking gardaí.'

*

When Tony Brady's car pulled up outside the funeral parlour, the scene before his eyes reminded him of one of those scenes from a classic Mafia movie.

Noel Quigley and his detectives were standing outside the funeral parlour, upright and formal and silent, like a bunch of FBI shits waiting for someone of importance to be pallbeared out.

Tony's own detective escort pulled up behind him. As soon as Tony got out of his car, they got out of theirs.

Reaching the door of the funeral parlour, Tony looked back at the gardaí standing all around, shaking his head with a disgusted sigh. 'Fuck's sake.'

As soon as he had disappeared inside, Noel Quigley's mind continued its focus on this latest irregularity from Michael Lynch.

A funeral parlour? Hardly the most cheerful place to meet a pal.

But then... Quigley's eyebrows twitched thoughtfully. Lynch and the rest of his gang hadn't been getting on so well lately...

*

Inside, Finbar directed Tony across the hallway to the storeroom, where he found Michael examining caskets.

'What the hell are you doing?'

Michael answered without looking round. 'This is a nice coffin, isn't it?'

'Yeah, lovely.'

'I've already ordered it. What do you think? Did I make the right choice? It's a bit dear, but what the hell. You only die once.'

Tony snapped, 'Give us a break, will you.'

Michael turned and looked him clear in the face. 'I've been fucking you about lately, haven't I, Tony?'

'You have, Michael. That's what you've been doing, all right.'

'I was out of order. I'm sorry.'

Tony shrugged. 'It's all right.'

'But whatever Stevie is up to now will only make things worse,' Michael warned. 'You know that, don't you?'

'No, I don't,' Tony snapped. 'He's only trying to sort things out. Get us back to where we were.'

'And that's just what Jerome Higgins wants.'

Tony was feeling uncomfortable. Michael seemed so certain. 'What choice have we? And you're not helping us at all.'

They were standing near the window. Noel Quigley and his colleague were peering in at them.

'Would you say any of those fellas can lip-read?' Michael murmured. 'You'd be amazed the skills the gardaí have these days.'

He moved up close to the window and pronounced his words very deliberately. 'Ye're ... fan-tas-tic ... lads ... do ... you ... know ... that?' And he kept on smiling.

'Michael —'

'Okay. Okay.' Michael turned away from the window. 'Look, just do one thing for me, Tony. Tell me what's next.'

'How d'you mean?'

'Stevie's going to try and get the painting to Higgins, right? With or without me.'

Tony didn't answer.

'Come on, Tony, we all know that. How does he think you'll get away from the gardaí to do it?'

'It's a good plan,' Tony said. 'I think it'll work.'

'Fair enough. So what's the plan?'

Tony shook his head, and stuffed his hands in his pockets.

'Trust me, will you.'

Tony hesitated for a moment, then concluded that of course he could trust Michael; they had been friends and accomplices all their lives.

'Do you know Copeland Grove?' Tony asked.

'Yeah.'

'It's a cul-de-sac, right? With steps at the end.'

'Leading on to Summerhill,' Michael said. 'You're going to drive up there? How, though? All together? One car's no good.'

'No. A car each, enough to block the road. That should give us enough time to get up the road to Summerhill.'

'When?'

'Tomorrow.'

'That soon? So what's the plan?'

Michael listened silently as Tony revealed to him every detail of Stevie's plan, and what he heard made his blood run cold.

Yet he knew that nothing he said would stop them. But at least he could try and warn Tony, if nothing else.

'Yeah, you'll get away from the gardaí. I bet you will, easily,' Michael said, when Tony had finished. 'Because I think they'll have been tipped off.'

'What?' Tony almost laughed. 'Tipped off — by who?'

'Look, which is better for Higgins? He buys a painting he can't get rid of — or he has all of Michael Lynch's gang arrested in one go, leaving just me to be dealt with in his own good time.'

Tony looked conflicted. After a silence, he had decided. 'No, Michael, I disagree with you. We're going in with Stevie on this. And I think you're wrong about Higgins.'

'Okay; believe me, don't believe me.' Michael shrugged. 'All I'm saying is to watch very carefully. But, as you've decided on doing this without me, at least let me give you a few helpful tips.'

Chapter twenty-five

Tony's head was throbbing with anxiety. He hadn't slept much the night before, and he was still pissed off at Michael for his sneering mistrust and for trying to put doubts in his mind.

It was a good plan. Even Alec had agreed on that. Stevie had worked the whole thing out in careful detail.

What Michael didn't seem to understand was that the Caravaggio meant nothing to any of them if it didn't bring them in money. All Michael seemed to want from the art robbery was the fame, whereas they were happy to fuck the fame and take the fortune.

Yet as he drove his car to the assembly point, hands on the wheel and eyes staring straight ahead, Tony couldn't shake Michael's words from his mind.

'So you're gonna drive your cars up Copeland Grove? A fucking cul-de-sac! *With a squad of detectives following you!'*

Tony glanced back and saw the usual squad of unmarked police cars right on his tail. He looked forward, to where Stevie was driving the car directly in front of him. Alec was driving the car ahead of Stevie.

They were approaching Copeland Grove.

Yeah, it seemed a crazy thing to do — drive up a street closed off at the far end, a route leading nowhere, a road from which there was no other escape for a car but the main entry.

But that was the beauty of the plan — Stevie's plan. Even Michael had seen some sense in it.

'A car each, enough to block the road... Yeah, not bad — if you can work it right.'

Tony tensed in readiness. Alec's car was now turning into Copeland Grove, Stevie's car behind him... Tony turned the wheel and followed them.

He glanced at the rear-view mirror and smiled. The line of unmarked cars were also turning into Copeland Grove, a quiet residential street. Tony could just imagine what the puzzled detectives were thinking: *What the hell's going on? Do they know someone who lives here?*

As Alec's car neared the top of the street, he gave the signal by suddenly turning his car into a spin. Stevie and Tony both turned swiftly, so that the three cars together blocked the road and pavement.

All three of them jumped out and began to run to the top of the street. Copeland Grove might be a cul-de-sac for cars, but it had a narrow pathway of pedestrian steps leading out of it.

The detectives skidded their cars to a halt, unable to give chase fast enough, as they were forced to clamber over the gang's three cars in order to get to the steps at the top.

The steps led to Summerhill Street, where the Hiace van was parked. Alec jumped behind the wheel and had the engine gunned in two seconds. Tony and Stevie jumped in the back, slamming the door as Alec zoomed away.

'We did it!' Stevie laughed, punching Tony's arm jubilantly. 'I told you we'd get away from the fuckers!'

Tony also laughed, full of relief; but then Michael's

voice came back into his head to spoil it all.

'Yeah, you'll get away from the gardaí. I bet you will, easily. Because I think they'll have been tipped off.'

Tipped off — stupid. Tony had looked back and seen with his own eyes just how fast those detectives had moved to give chase.

'Look! This is not Stevie's plan, it's Jerome Higgins's plan... And which is better for Higgins? He buys a painting he can't get rid of — or he has all of Michael Lynch's gang arrested in one go, leaving just me to be dealt with in his own good time... Believe me, don't believe me. All I'm saying is to watch very carefully...'

Stevie was talking animatedly about the rest of the plan, but once again Tony was beginning to feel un-comfortable and a little uncertain.

'When you get in that van, make sure you can see everything that's going on around you. Think about it: Higgins or Stevie — who would the smart money be on?'

Tony moved closer to the back window of the van.

'As soon as you take off, an unmarked car will appear from somewhere, nice and casual. Then you'll know, Tony. You'll know Higgins has set you all up. It's all I'm asking — look out for that car.'

Tony watched very carefully, but he could see no car; nothing was following them.

Tony slowly relaxed. The fact was, Michael was way off-beam about Jerome Higgins, had always despised him, and all because of Billy and the drugs. Higgins had been Billy's heroin pusher and cocaine dealer, and Michael would never forgive him for that.

Stevie nudged Tony's arm. 'You listening to me?'

'Yeah.'

Stevie grinned happily. 'See, the way me and Higgins see it, if we're reasonable, we can divide up the work.

Co-operate. We let each other know what we're doing, that kind of thing. You know, so we don't get in each other's way. In fact, the opposite.'

Tony stared at him in disbelief, realisation dawning. So this *was* Higgins's plan, after all — not Stevie's.

'This'll be the kind of job Higgins says we'll be able to get in on,' Stevie continued. 'We're finally getting rid of the painting, right? A hundred grand, right? So now, while we have the filth running around like blue-arsed flies wondering where we're gone, Higgins will have some of his crowd robbing the bank on Dame Street.'

'What!' Tony blinked his eyes. 'I can't believe what I'm hearing.'

'And, listen, he's promised me a cut of that — the bank job — on top of the hundred grand for the painting. That's just for us three, the hundred grand, and none for Michael. I mean, like, it's *brilliant*! Two scams happening at the same time — the filth won't know where to look. They won't be able to handle it. And it'll work better for all of us.'

Through the back window, Tony saw a car appear. It seemed to have come out of nowhere, and it was following them up the road... Was that Noel Quigley in the front passenger seat? Or was he just imagining it?

Michael's words came back to haunt him. *'What do you do if I'm right? What d'you think? You get the fuck out of that van as fast as you can.'*

Tony's heart was pounding; he couldn't make up his mind what to do. He looked at Stevie jabbering away, madly excited.

He looked back at the car pursuing them, almost sure now that it was Noel Quigley in the passenger seat.

'Stop the van, Alec!' Tony shouted. 'There's a car behind us.'

'Yeah, so? In case you haven't noticed,' Alec quipped, 'we're, like, on a road, Tony.'

'I think it's the guards.'

Stevie peered out the window, and Tony peered with him. The car had dropped back...

Stevie shrugged. 'You're just a bit jittery, that's all.'

No, Tony was certain now. The way the car had quickly dropped back when his face had appeared at the van window was the big give-away.

'Listen,' he said to Stevie, 'we haven't collected the painting yet, so even if we are stopped by the guards, we're in the clear. We've nothing on us, so what can they do? We can always work out our own plan for another day.'

'No fucking way,' Stevie retorted. 'We couldn't have a better day than this. Don't you understand — weren't you *listening* to me? Right now Jerome Higgins is staging a bank robbery to divert the gardaí's attention from us. They'll all be heading to Dame Street this minute on a bank-robbery alert. Higgins is taking a major risk so's to give us a clear run to get the painting for him.'

Tony suspected the opposite was probably true — Higgins was using them to divert the police from the bank robbery.

He looked through the window and saw the car still on their tail, and someone who looked like Noel Quigley still in the passenger seat. And it could have been his imagination, but he was sure the long line of unmarked cars following it were also police.

He leaned forward and yelled, 'Stop the van, Alec!'

Alec glanced back. 'No way! We've got to keep moving fast, Tony, you know that. So no fucking way am I stopping!'

But he had to stop seconds later, at traffic lights. Tony bashed open the back doors of the van and sprang out.

'Yous can be Higgins's fall guys if you want, but not me!'

He slammed the van doors closed and ran like mad, disappearing down a side-street — Michael's words ringing through his head...

'And as soon as you get away, Tony, phone me ... or don't, if you like. It's your choice. But I promise, I'll be waiting.'

Chapter twenty-Six

Two of the detectives detailed to guard and follow Michael Lynch had the resonating names of Liam and Larry.

They had been sitting outside Michael Lynch's house since early morning, and now they were truly fed up. Liam got out of the car to stretch his legs again and have another smoke. Larry remained in the car, reading his book.

Liam was the ambitious one, young and full of energy and restless for a result. He smoked his cigarette down to the butt, and lit up another; Larry didn't like him smoking in the car. He stood blowing out smoke while looking at the house. No sign of Lynch all day. The only visitor had been the sister-in-law, and she was still inside.

*

Christine and Lisa were sitting in the kitchen drinking tea when the telephone rang. Michael picked it up in the hall.

'Yeah?'

'Michael, it's Tony... You were right, it's a fuck-up.'

'Okay, calm down. Are you free? There's no one following you?'

'No. I'm in town now — Dorset Street.'

'So did you find out anything? Where's Higgins supposed to pick up the painting?'

'He's doing better than that,' Tony said. 'Higgins is going to pull a bank job at the same time the painting is supposed to be collected. A bank job in town — while half the gardaí in Dublin are chasing Stevie and Alec up the mountains.'

'Where — do you know?'

'Yeah, Dame Street.'

Michael shook his head, anger consuming him. If Jerome Higgins wasn't the biggest betrayer since Judas —

'Okay, listen. Go there now. To Dame Street. Fast. Check it out. But make sure you're not being followed. Ring me from there in fifteen minutes. What are you wearing, by the way?'

'What?'

Michael's mind was already devising a plan. 'I need to know what you're wearing.'

'Blue jeans, red shirt, wax jacket — you know the one.'

'Good. Talk to you in fifteen minutes.'

Michael put down the phone.

He could see and hear Christine and Lisa still chatting in the kitchen. He turned and ran upstairs to the bedroom, alert and animated, his own plan becoming clearer in his head.

He changed his clothes — blue jeans, red shirt. He and Tony often bought similar clothes, but never wore them at the same social occasions. It was a habit that had served them well in the past.

He opened a drawer and took out a gun, checked it was loaded. He took out another gun and emptied it. Fifteen minutes later he was ready and waiting when the telephone rang again.

'Tony?'

'Yeah. Everything normal in the bank so far. Maybe Stevie was bullshitting.'

Michael said, 'I don't think so. I think we're in business. Okay, Tony, are you listening?'

'Yeah.'

'Here's what's going to happen. Once you see me coming, you go inside the bank and hang around. I'll wait outside. As soon as Higgins and his boys arrive, we're off and running.'

'What about the gardaí?'

'Just as Higgins planned — most of them will be following Alec and Stevie all the way to the Caravaggio.'

*

Alec and Stevie had reached the warehouse. Stevie was still shocked at Tony's action.

'I mean — and you saw it, Alec — there was no car tailing us, just ordinary traffic. It was all in his mind.'

Alec nodded. 'Look, stop babbling and get out and open the warehouse doors, will you.'

Stevie got out of the Hiace and unlocked and opened the warehouse doors. Alec swung the van inside.

'Right, now up to the office to get the painting,' Stevie said eagerly. 'Then straight on to Wicklow.'

*

Tony held the phone to his ear, feeling bad and wanting to apologise to Michael for ever doubting him.

'Michael —'

'See you in the bank, Tony — soon.'

Michael put down the phone and turned to see

Christine and Lisa standing behind him.

Christine said, 'Well?'

'Well what?'

'Have you two kissed and made up?'

'Me and Tony? Yeah, sure.'

'Good. You can't be falling out with friends like him.'

Michael paused for a long moment. 'Listen ... I think I'll be able to fix things.' He grinned. 'You know, so you're not left walking the streets begging.'

Lisa said, 'Course you will.'

Christine glanced at her. 'We're not worried, are we?'

'Not a bit.'

Michael nodded. 'Yeah, but ... it's been on my mind. And I just wanted you to know ... I'm looking after things.'

Neither of the women understood what he was trying to say to them. Both were too full of relief that he was friends with Tony Brady again. Long years of experience had taught them that Michael truly loved three things: he loved life, he loved his two families, and he loved his gang.

And maybe now he would sort it out with Stevie and Alec, too. Because, whatever the problems, Stevie and Alec were two great lads underneath, and they had shared so much with Michael over the years. This was just a hiccup, both women were sure of that. Before long they'd all be great pals again.

*

Michael mounted the Kawasaki and sped away from the house. Liam and Larry were right on his tail, tracking him all the way into town, just as Michael had known they would.

On Dame Street he drew the bike to a halt, across the

road from the bank, then sat back and waited.

Liam and Larry pulled in behind him. They looked at each other, bewildered. 'What's he doing? Why's he stopped here?'

To find out, the only thing they could do was the same thing he was doing: sit and wait.

Michael suddenly tensed. A car was pulling up outside the bank. He noticed it instantly because of the driver — Shay Kirby.

So Higgins had got to him too. The realisation made Michael feel a little sick. He also felt sad and regretful, because he had not only liked Shay Kirby, he had trusted him. Too bad that Shay had made such a disastrous error of judgement, at this late stage in the game, by teaming up with the wrong man. His new boss would be dead before nightfall.

Two IRA men slid out of the back seat of the car and walked swiftly into the bank. Only two — and neither was Jerome Higgins.

So Higgins had to be already inside, Michael realised.

He smiled grimly to himself as he got off the bike: his day with Jerome Higgins had come at last.

He ran across the road to the bank, tapping Shay's window as he passed, letting him know he was on the scene.

Shay Kirby bolted upright and stared after him, disbelieving.

'See that?' Liam had also jolted upright as soon as Lynch got off his motorbike. 'See him rapping on the window of that car there?'

The two detectives stared at Shay Kirby, who was completely unaware of their presence in the unmarked car.

As soon as Michael entered the bank, he caught Tony's eye. He nodded towards the two IRA men, and Tony understood.

Michael turned away and picked up a pen, pretending to fill in a payment slip while covertly watching the two IRA men. They had now been joined by a third man, who casually walked up to them from the far end of the bank — Jerome Higgins.

*

Outside, Shay Kirby had jumped out of the car to follow Lynch into the bank, unaware of the two detectives walking quickly towards him.

At the bank's entrance, Shay hesitated, not really sure what he should do. He was supposed to be ready and waiting at the wheel when Higgins and the others ran out, and if he cocked that up...

No, he decided, best to go back to the car and stick to his orders.

Shay turned — and came face to face with the two detectives. Instantly he knew they were police and made to run, but they were on him, jumping all over him as he fell back onto the ground — fucking smothering him!

Liam and Larry pulled him to his feet, handcuffed him, then dragged him struggling over to their car and shoved him inside.

'Better ask for assistance,' Liam decided, and went to his radio. 'Control, Foxtrot 1 calling. Request urgent assistance. We have a situation here.'

'Foxtrot 1 — are you off your head? Urgent assistance? With six armed units chasing after that fucking painting?'

*

Inside the bank, the three IRA men suddenly tugged on balaclavas and pulled out their guns — causing the usual panic and screaming, until everyone was ordered to lie on the floor.

'Face down! On the floor, face down! This is a raid!' They threatened to shoot anyone who moved.

Michael dropped face down like all the other customers. Tony did the same. They glanced at each other across the floor, waiting patiently as the robbery commenced.

Michael couldn't help wondering about Stevie and Alec.

*

Because Michael Lynch had never informed them other-wise, Stevie and Alec had no idea that the painting which hung on the wall in Michael's office was a replica. No one in the world knew that, except Michael himself. He had never believed in playing with an open hand. Even with his gang, all information was given on a need-to-know basis only.

Stevie and Alec carefully lifted the painting off the wall, thinking it was Caravaggio's original — worth thirty million.

'Course, Tony was supposed to be up here helping me do this,' Stevie said sullenly to Alec, 'while you stayed below with the engine running. Can you believe he let us down like that?'

Alec was in too bad a mood to discuss it. Tony's action had unnerved him slightly. 'Come on, let's get this thing shifted.'

'All right, all right — but, you know, I'm only saying...' Stevie babbled on as they carried the painting out of the office and along the upper landing, to the stairs.

*

Down below, in the shadows of the warehouse, Noel Quigley and a squad of detectives waited, all heavily armed. They had followed the Hiace all the way, and now it seemed the tip-off had been sound.

On the landing above, they could see *The Taking of Christ* moving before their eyes, being carried by two men whom they could not see, hidden as they were behind the huge, framed canvas.

Now they were in clear range. Noel Quigley gave the signal, and the entire armed unit stepped out, pointing their guns upwards.

'Stop where you are!' Quigley shouted. 'You have no chance of escape!'

Alec's face popped round the frame, his eyes boggling with shock. He drew back again and stared at Stevie.

'Fuck you! Michael wouldn't have got us into this mess.'

Stevie was just as horror-struck. 'What the fuck'll we do?'

Alec suddenly remembered what had happened in the National Gallery. 'As long as we stay behind the painting, they can't touch us. No way are they going to fire their guns and destroy a precious piece of art.'

'So what'll we do?' Stevie's mind had lost all its initiative.

'Make our way down to the van behind the cover of the painting,' Alec said. 'Just like we did in the art gallery.'

Noel Quigley stared as the painting started to move again, the men still behind it, and suddenly he too realised what was happening. Once again Michael Lynch had the gardaí by the balls, and the Caravaggio was going to help him and his gang get clear away again.

The armed unit were looking to Quigley for instructions.

'Fuck art!' Quigley suddenly shouted, raising his automatic rifle and firing like a madman.

The armed unit followed his lead.

The explosion of gunfire in the warehouse was deafening. The Caravaggio painting toppled backwards onto the ground, bullet-ridden. Stevie and Alec lay dead beneath it.

Chapter Twenty-Seven

'**D**on't mess with me, fuckface!' Higgins warned a teller who was slow in bagging his money. 'This is the IRA you're dealing with.'

All the bank staff were terrified, doing what they had to do as fast as they could.

And the IRA won't see a penny of it, Michael thought. Higgins was using the political name for his own private gain.

Five minutes later, the three robbers were backing away towards the main entrance of the bank. Michael and Tony were watching each other across the floor.

Michael winked — and pulled out his gun. So did Tony.

One robber was shot dead instantly. The second was wounded in the leg but still ran from the bank, shooting wildly.

The third almost made it to the door, but Michael had already sprung into action. He grabbed him from behind, holding the robber's neck in an armlock. With his other hand he pressed his gun against the balaclava and cocked the hammer. 'Drop the gun. Drop it!'

The sawn-off shotgun was dropped onto the floor. Michael kicked it aside, then ripped off the balaclava.

Michael's smile was both relieved and malevolent.

'Ah, good — it's you, Jerome. For a second there I thought you'd got away.'

Once again, Higgins gave him the dirtiest look he had ever seen. 'Did Stevie Brady grass me?'

'No, you fucked Stevie, set him up, and for that I'm going to make you pay, Higgins.'

Michael moved back a few paces and picked up the sawn-off shotgun. 'Or maybe I'll just take you hostage and let Stevie blow your fucking head off.'

'We can still do a deal, Lynch.'

'Like the deal you did with my brother Billy? Everyone who does a deal with you ends up the loser, don't they, Jerome?'

Michael's face was full of hatred, and for the first time Higgins's face showed real fear. He had not only messed with the crime boss's gang, he had fucked up his brother, one of his family; and everyone knew how Lynch felt about his family.

'Get over to the counter and sit down with your back to it!' Michael ordered. 'Come on, move — *move*!'

Higgins backed over to the counter and sat down.

'Spread your legs out in front of you and put your hands on your head.'

As Higgins did as he was told, he began to plead, 'Take the money, Michael, all of it — just let me get out.'

Michael looked at him intently with his dark eyes and said quietly, 'Jerome, there's no way you're getting out of this.'

*

Liam couldn't believe his luck. First they'd captured the driver of the getaway car — and now one of the robbers had run out of the bank and collapsed straight into his arms, blood spilling down his leg.

Liam dragged him over to the car, where Larry was guarding Shay Kirby. 'Another one to go in,' Liam said, opening the door. 'But, God, we've *got* to get some fucking assistance!'

A crowd had gathered outside the bank. Liam kept his eyes on the bank's entrance while talking into his radio.

'Control, there is an armed robbery in progress. Must have urgent assistance. Lynch is involved. This is a highly dangerous situation.'

'Doing our best. I have some unarmed units on their way.'

'For fuck's sake, we need *armed* assistance urgently! There's only two of us. There's three men, armed and dangerous, in there. One of them is Michael Lynch, do you understand?'

*

Detective Sergeant Noel Quigley was still in the warehouse. Gerard Murphy had lifted up the destroyed Caravaggio.

Noel couldn't care less about the two dead men on the floor, but now it was all over, his rationality was returning, and he knew he would be in big trouble over this. The masterpiece in ruins, the loss to the nation...

Gerard Murphy read his thoughts and tried to make a joke. He grinned, 'I hope they don't take the cost of it out of your wages, Noel.'

One of the detectives from a car outside ran into the warehouse and shouted up a message.

'Sorry, Noel, getting urgent calls — an armed robbery in progress at a bank on Dame Street. They're still inside. One of them is Michael Lynch.'

A flash of cold light seemed to freeze Noel's eyes; he stood staring at the detective as if struck blind. 'What...?'

'They're desperate to have the assistance of armed units. If we don't move fast, Lynch will get away. He's armed and they're not.'

Noel came out of his shock, white-faced and furious.

'Tell them to keep Lynch there!' he roared, already running towards the stairs. 'All units move fast, and you — radio back and tell them I don't care how they do it, but somehow they must *keep Lynch there until I arrive*!'

*

Tony Brady was stuffing bags of money inside his jacket. He picked up a few more thick wads of notes and stuffed them into the various pockets in his jeans. Dressed as he was, he looked just like Michael.

'Okay, I'm ready.' Tony adjusted his balaclava and put on the motorcycle helmet.

'Now we have to make them think I'm surrendering,' Michael said. He quickly unzipped Tony's jacket a few inches, pulled out five wads of notes — five grand — and stuffed them inside his own jacket.

'This is your big moment, Tony, because they don't know about you at all. No one saw you coming in here.'

He handed Tony the key for the Kawasaki. 'Take a look at where my bike is out there.'

Tony looked.

'You go out, arms up, surrendering. They'll take you over to their car, just behind the bike. Whatever you do, don't let the detectives find out it's not me until you reach the car. Remember, they haven't really got a clue what's happening — and they've got two prisoners to watch out there already. They're terrified —'

'Sure, but listen to me for a second...' Tony desperately wanted to apologise to Michael for mistrusting him, deserting him. 'What I want to say —'

'I'll be watching,' Michael continued his instructions. 'When I see you at the car, I'll start a diversion — and that's when you have to run.'

'Yeah, but what'll you do?'

'Don't ask stupid questions — just trust me.'

'Yeah, I do trust you. But I don't see how —'

Jerome Higgins made a move. Michael was on him in seconds, the gun pressed against his skull.

'I thought you IRA fellas had stopped wanting to be martyrs!' he snapped. 'Another move, Higgins, and I'll finish you right here.'

Higgins looked at him. Both knew it was not a threat, but a deadly serious promise.

Michael moved backwards a pace, to Tony. 'Will you stop arguing and go! Otherwise you'll get us both killed.'

He opened the bank's door a fraction and shouted out to the street, 'Hey, lads — Michael Lynch talking to you! Can you hear me?'

Liam jerked alert. 'Yes.'

'I'm coming out. I'm giving myself up, okay? So what do you want me to do?'

Liam could hardly believe it! Life was shooting a big dollop of luck straight into his hands. At this rate, he'd have it all sewn up before Quigley arrived.

'Right, then,' Liam shouted back, now in full command. 'I want you to hold up your hands clearly in the air and come out slowly. Keep walking towards us until I tell you to stop.'

Michael shouted back, 'Okay, here I come, lads. Yous fellas are going to be heroes, d'you know that?'

He winked at Tony and whispered, 'Relax — eye on the ball.'

'And if I do get away, Michael, what happens to you?'

Michael smiled ruefully. 'Ah, Tony, you don't expect
me to have *all* the answers, do you?'

Tony looked at him anxiously, then nodded. 'Okay,
here I go.' He raised his hands in the air and slowly
walked out.

A gasp went up from the crowd as the notorious
Michael Lynch walked out of the bank with his hands
high in the air.

The two detectives sprang and grabbed an arm each,
marching him over to their car. Although they tried not to
show it, they were both very frightened.

'Okay, what's going on, Lynch? Who's left in there?'

They had reached the car.

'Right, get that helmet and balaclava off,' Liam
commanded. 'It's the last time you'll wear them.'

Tony glanced towards the Kawasaki.

'Fuck you!' Liam shouted. 'It's coming off whether you
like it or not!' He reached up and pulled the helmet off,
then yanked back the balaclava.

Tony grinned at him. 'Hello, how're yeh?'

Liam looked at Larry, unable to believe it. He'd been
shot up the arse for a fool and not even realised it.

Michael opened the bank's door with a terrifying roar,
firing at the detectives.

Both dived for cover. Tony jumped over the bonnet of
the car and ran to the Kawasaki, leaped on it and revved.
Seeing their chance, the two IRA men in the car also tried
to break loose, kicking the car door open. The two
detectives jumped to their feet and grabbed them.

Amidst the pandemonium outside, Michael saw Tony
zoom away. He swung round to Jerome Higgins and
yanked him to his feet, pulling him clear of the other
customers and bank staff, holding the gun to his head.

'Right, everyone, up ye get!' Michael shouted. 'One by

one, and walk out with your hands held high.'

The customers on the floor raised their heads and stared at him.

'Come on, move it! I'm setting you free, folks. Don't waste my time.'

Slightly in shock, the staff and customers began to move to their feet, one by one, as Michael motioned them outside. They went like scared rabbits, expecting to be shot at any moment.

*

Noel Quigley's car and two armed response units arrived at the scene as the hostages emerged from the bank with hands raised, calling out in terror to the detectives.

'Don't shoot!'

'No, don't shoot! We're innocent bystanders!'

'We were just in the bank to —'

'All right, all right, get a fucking move on!' Liam and Larry were trying to drag the customers out of harm's way when Noel reached them.

'What's happening?'

'I haven't a clue,' Liam replied, 'but Lynch is still in there.'

'Is he now!' Noel ran back to the armed units and ordered them into position — they had arrived just in time. *'Lynch is still in the bank.'*

And that was when Noel Quigley made his decision.

Somehow he had to justify the elaborate surveillance he had organised for so long now, the cost to the force, the ruined Caravaggio... Lynch had outmanoeuvred him at every turn, failed to fall into the various traps, but now he had his chance to strike back.

And it could be his *only* chance. Lynch was inside the

bank, caught red-handed in a crime for which he would be put away for at least ten years. But maybe not. Who ever knew, with Lynch? He and his crooked lawyers might find some way to get him off.

And that would be the end of any promotion for Noel Quigley. After spending a fortune in overtime wages, the force would be back to where it had started, and Michael Lynch would still be a menace to society.

Coldly and calmly, Noel Quigley decided to take out Michael Lynch in one simple tactical manoeuvre. All the conditions were perfect, and such an opportunity as this one, he knew, might never come again.

*

Michael, hidden from view, was watching from the open door of the bank. As soon as he saw Noel Quigley arrive, he sprang into action.

He too was determined on a bloody act of retribution.

He pulled a balaclava out of his pocket and handed it to Jerome Higgins. 'Put it on.'

Michael moved Higgins near to the bank's door, keeping the gun trained close to his head as he watched Higgins put the balaclava on.

'Good man. Now I want you to have this.' He took the emptied gun from his jacket and shoved it into Higgins's hand. 'Now get the fuck out!'

Before Higgins could even react, Michael had pushed him out the door. And suddenly the whole street went deadly still as Michael Lynch appeared in the doorway of the bank.

The armed units were at the ready. Noel Quigley called out from behind the cover of his car. 'Put your hands up, Lynch! Then come forward slowly.'

Higgins raised his hands to rip off the hood, show them he was not Michael Lynch — but one of the hands he raised had a gun in it.

As soon as Higgins raised his hands, Michael, watching from the bank, fired a wild shot.

Noel Quigley couldn't believe Lynch had played into his hands so easily. He reacted to the shot immediately — firing his rifle straight at the balaclava.

He saw Michael Lynch almost blown away as the armed units opened fire. The crumpled body lying on the ground was soaked in blood.

It was just fantastic.

'Great!' Noel whispered.

*

An eerie silence had descended on the street. Noel walked over to the blood-soaked body. Lynch had taken numerous shots to the head. The balaclava, once black, was now dark red.

But something was wrong.

Noel suddenly thought — frowned — tried to remember... Surely there had been a shot from the bank, drawing the police fire. Was he imagining it?

He walked past the body and into the bank. The place was empty and silent.

He called out, 'Lynch! ... Lynch!'

The words were just a hollow echo. Michael Lynch was dead on the pavement outside, and he, Noel Quigley, had done the job he had promised everyone he would do.

Yet... Quigley could not deny his own intelligence. There *had* been a shot fired from the bank, a definite shot, fired only seconds before the man lying dead outside had had his face blown away.

Maybe that was what Lynch had planned? To make people think he was dead, believe he was dead? And what would be the consequences of that?

Noel's mind quickly assessed the situation again. For himself, it would be the end of his career in the gardaí. No more promotion, nothing. So far his operation had cost the force a fortune in extra resources — the huge number of detectives on twenty-four-hour surveillance. Two of Lynch's gang had been shot dead in the warehouse, another lay dead on the street outside. Then there was the cost to the country itself, the Caravaggio original — against every strict order, he had damaged one of the great art treasures of the world, ripped it to shreds with bullets. The act of a madman? Or of a police officer under threat, doing his duty?

But if Michael Lynch was still alive, still free...?

A slight sound behind him — Quigley swung round and stared. From somewhere on high, a few five-pound notes were swirling down to the ground. He looked up sharply, swiftly, all around the ceiling; there was nowhere the notes could have come from.

He swallowed, his mind rationalising: banknotes had flown all over the place in the chaos, so it must have been a whiff of wind from the open door that had dislodged these few... He was nervous, that was all.

Then he saw the ventilation shaft, in the far corner of the ceiling; his attention was caught by another five-pound note floating down from it. Noel felt a sinking sensation as he watched it.

If — if Lynch had outmanoeuvred him again... It would ruin him... But only if anyone else knew.

No, he could not, would not let a scumbag like Michael Lynch ruin him.

Noel Quigley was filled with a cold rage as he made his

decision. It was a disgusting decision for a police officer, but in the end everyone had to look after Number One.

He stared hard at the ventilation shaft and almost spat with venom as he announced his judgement. 'You're dead, Lynch, do you hear me? From now on, you're dead. And you'll stay dead! *Dead!*'

Not a sound answered him. Maybe he was talking only to himself, and Lynch really was dead outside.

The silence was broken by the wailing of police sirens approaching the bank. Quigley gave one last look around, then turned to go.

Liam appeared in the doorway. 'Sir, is that it?'

Noel looked at the young detective and nodded, his voice clear and calm. 'Yes, that's it. Contact Lynch's wife. Ask her to come and identify her husband's body. No, don't ask her — *tell* her she has to come. Understood?'

Liam nodded. 'Understood, sir.'

*

A short time later, when the cars and the crowd had gone, Michael Lynch walked carefully along a roof-ladder to another building and freedom.

Chapter twenty-eight

The knocking on the front door was so loud, Christine thought it was the gardaí.

She threw a glance of caution at Lisa, then squared her shoulders and walked down the hall to open the door.

Tony half-staggered inside, the bulk of his jacket weighed down with money.

Christine stared at him blankly, surprised; but when he went into the living-room, unzipped his jacket and let wads of notes spill onto the sofa, she finally understood.

'That's where he went, then?' she said. 'On a job?'

Tony nodded. 'The bank in Dame Street.'

'So where is he now?'

Tony wondered if he could lie to her, but there was really no point. 'I don't know, Christine. Last I seen him, he was still inside the bank.'

Christine looked at him darkly. 'On his own?'

'No — I don't know, like; I'm not certain... I couldn't work out what he was up to. All I know is that he got me out of there, and told me to come straight here and give you this.' He pointed to the money. 'I'll take a few grand for myself, but the rest is yours.'

'Mine?'

'Well, for both of you,' Tony said, glancing at Lisa.

'And since when has any money from a job been mine or Lisa's?' Christine asked, now certain something was very wrong.

Tony looked as uneasy as she felt. 'Now, I don't know what his thinking was, Christine; all I know is what he asked me to do.'

The telephone in the hall rang. Lisa went to answer it.

'Yes... What?... Yes... Oh, Jesus, no...'

She dropped the receiver and walked into the living-room, staring at Christine.

'That was the gardaí. They want ... they want you to go down and identify Michael's body.'

Christine lost her breath. She wavered for a moment, her mind going black, then she felt Tony and Lisa holding on to her.

*

Lisa was still holding on to her when they both entered the mortuary. Commissioner Daly and Detective Sergeant Quigley were already there, waiting.

Commissioner Daly organised his manner and voice to show some respect for the legal widow. The other slut — the sister — he did not even condescend to acknowledge.

He looked solicitously at Christine. 'Are you Michael Lynch's wife?'

Christine did not look in his direction or answer him. Even now, she would not break the code of never talking to gardaí.

Commissioner Daly sighed. He had got the message.

'Right,' he said. 'Will you formally identify this body as that of your husband, Michael Lynch? A nod will do.'

An attendant was standing by the sheeted corpse. He

drew it down slowly to reveal the face, and both women let out a gasp of horror. The right eye had been shot away, the socket caked in blood; the nose and both cheekbones were smashed to pulp. The entire face was unrecognisable.

Lisa almost fainted, but this time it was Christine who drew up her strength. She was appalled at the gardaí's lack of sensitivity and respect, even if she was a criminal's wife.

'Oh God, yes, I'm sorry,' Commissioner Daly said in genuine apology. 'I should have warned you beforehand. But perhaps ... some identifying marks on the body?'

The attendant drew down the sheet to reveal the naked body. Noel Quigley held his breath as the two women stared. They stood with their backs to him, so he could not see their faces.

They stood staring for a long time.

'Can you identify this body as that of your husband?' Commissioner Daly asked quietly.

Christine drew a long breath, then gave her answer directly to the attendant.

'Yes. This is the body of my husband, Michael Lynch,' she said, then turned to leave. She walked past Daly and Quigley as if they did not exist.

Lisa, who had paused to take one last look at the body, turned also and silently left the mortuary.

Commissioner Daly gave Noel Quigley a smile of triumph. 'Right, it's over. He's been identified by his wife. Now you can get on with the paperwork.'

Noel Quigley was feeling weak with relief.

Commissioner Daly patted him on the shoulder and said sincerely, 'Well done, Noel.'

*

'Jesus, I need a brandy.'

Christine and Lisa headed straight for the nearest pub. Both were still stunned, but delighted too.

No way was that Michael's body. The shoulders weren't broad enough, the hair on the chest was too skimpy and not black enough, and the stomach was too flat. Everything about it was wrong, because it was the wrong body.

Christine took a large swig of brandy and laughed. 'As soon as I saw that poor prick on the slab, I knew it wasn't Michael.'

'I'll kill Michael for putting us through this,' Lisa said. 'What in God's name is he up to?'

Christine shook her head; she didn't know what he was up to, and she didn't care. He was alive, and that was the only thing that mattered to her. He was alive.

She took another swig of brandy, emptying the glass. 'But I'll tell you what I'd like to know,' she said. 'Where is he now?'

'Ah, sure...' Lisa slapped a fiver on the bar for two more drinks. 'Don't you know he'll show up when he's good and ready?'

Chapter twenty-nine

Finbar Sheridan sat in his little pantry, drinking tea and wondering who the man in the coffin was.

It was not Michael Lynch, that he knew. A late-night telephone call had informed him of that. But he would have known anyway. Finbar had spent years eyeing and sizing men up, unconsciously measuring them for their coffins — not through any ill feeling, but from simple force of habit.

It was a habit that often offered great benefit and comfort to the mourners, because once Finbar had seen a man healthy and happy in life, he used his skill to make him look so lifelike in his coffin that he looked as if he was just sleeping peacefully.

His greatest respect was reserved for the women. He never allowed a female corpse to lie naked in his embalming room; her private parts were always covered, *always*. Once he'd had an apprentice assisting him in the embalming room who had laughed and repeated a dirty joke he'd heard on the television the night before. Finbar had been so outraged by such lack of decorum and respect in front of a dead female, he had fired him on the spot.

There was so much more to the profession of being an undertaker than the technical skill; there was the respect of silence, the gentleness and care of the hands at work, and the quiet ritual of uttering encouraging words throughout. After all, life for everyone was miserable, death was a grand release, and only the lucky died young.

Yet, despite knowing all that and believing it firmly, Finbar was glad to know the dead man was not Michael, not his old pal. The years they had spent together in prison still gave him fond memories, and many of those memories still gave him a good laugh. So it was grand to think that they might meet up again sometime, somewhere, and have another few laughs.

Of course, if it ever came out that he, a registered and respected undertaker, had knowingly conspired in burying an unknown man documented and registered to be Michael Lynch, his reputation would be ruined and he would probably be put in jail.

But Finbar wasn't worried. He would plead innocence. The face had been destroyed beyond all recognition — and who was responsible for that? The bloody gardaí. And who had said the dead body was Michael Lynch? The bloody gardaí.

And then an amusing thought suddenly struck Finbar, making him chuckle. If it ever came out that Michael Lynch was *not* dead, but healthy and well and thriving, as strong as ever — who would look the jackasses and be ridiculed for weeks in the press? The bloody gardaí.

*

The funeral of Michael Lynch took place the following morning, seven days after the shooting.

Detective Sergeant Noel Quigley and three of his colleagues from the Central Detective Unit attended the funeral. Noel hadn't lowered himself to go to the funeral of Alec Duignan or Stevie Brady, but nothing would have kept him away from this event. Especially as most of the Irish media were present, and Noel was being regarded as some sort of hero — the man who had proved himself more than a match for the crime boss, Michael Lynch.

The detectives and reporters stood outside the church and watched the hearse drive up, followed by two black limousines containing the two 'wives' and their children.

As they piled out, the children didn't look sad; they had an air of frivolity, as if they were attending a wedding celebration or a First Communion. Noel felt a wave of anxiety stirring within him.

Then the widow stepped out. She was dressed in black — a colour that didn't suit her; but she looked heart-broken, her face squeezed up as if she was trying to stop herself from bursting into tears, rushing into the church to follow the coffin and avoid the cameras of the press.

Noel's anxiety soared into exhilaration. Perhaps Lynch *was* dead. It was something he would never know for sure. But the face of Christine Lynch had erased all his deepest fears. That woman was *grieving*.

Not that Noel felt any sympathy for her — nor for her sister, who looked just as grief-stricken, her head bowed as she pulled the children into the church.

After a further fifteen minutes, Noel realised that the Lynch funeral was going to be a small family affair. No other known criminals attended. The other detectives were very disappointed by that.

When the service began, the detectives and media moved inside to the back of the church and waited patiently for it to end. The reporters looked bored; it was a very simple service, with nothing unusual to report. No one stood up and gave an emotional reading or said a tearful eulogy.

Then suddenly music flared up, and a song began.

You left me when I needed you most...

Noel Quigley thought it outrageous music to play at a funeral — and blaring through loudspeakers, too.

You left without even closing the door.
I didn't stand in your way.
Now I need you more
Than I did before...

The press loved it. Even at his funeral, Michael Lynch's family had decided to be irreverent by playing a pop song.

'No,' Lisa explained passionately to them, when the service was over. 'That was Michael's favourite song. He always loved it. So why shouldn't we play it for him one last time?'

A huge crowd had gathered outside the church. Most were just common gawkers out to enjoy themselves at the funeral of a notorious criminal. Some of the young girls were unable to resist posing in front of the TV cameras. Some even threw flowers on the coffin as it was carried out of the church, while others had the audacity to wipe tears from their eyes. Noel turned away in disgust.

His colleague, Gerard Murphy, looked up at the sky with an ironical expression on his face.

'You know something?' he said. 'Lynch would love this send-off. He's probably up there somewhere having a big laugh at the idea of us being here protecting him.'

Noel's face was impassive as he watched the coffin being carried to the hearse. 'Right, let's get this over with.'

Gerard caught his arm, concerned. 'Listen, Noel,' he said quietly. 'You did your job, that's all. And you did the right thing, you know. We're all better off with him dead.'

Noel nodded. 'That's how it started, Gerard — just a job. But it turned into something between Lynch and me. Something personal. That's how these things usually end up.'

'Yeah, but he's dead now and soon he'll be six feet under. So don't give him another thought after today, okay? And, hey,' Gerard added, 'don't forget your promotion! That's something we have to celebrate. And my bet is on you getting Daly's job within five years.'

Noel smiled.

Chapter thirty

It had been a good summer in the Irish countryside. The fine weather had resulted in a wealth of crops, giving farmers a good harvest.

Michael Lynch was riding his Kawasaki through the county of Kerry. With the five grand he had shoved inside his jacket, in the bank, he had decided to take some time out and do a motorcycle tour of his own lovely country, stopping in small hotels along the way.

He drove into a small village and stopped at a general store which doubled as a post office. He needed to buy a postage stamp.

He took off his helmet and went inside.

The woman behind the counter was middle-aged, and a real countrywoman, her eyes showing keen interest at the sight of a stranger and the possibility of a good chat.

'Hello, there,' she said. 'Lovely day for it.'

Michael smiled. Country people always said it was a lovely day for it, but they never said *what*.

So he asked her, 'A lovely day for what?'

'For whatever you want to do,' she smiled.

'Yeah, well, I'm just touring,' he said, 'you know, enjoying the countryside.'

His eyes were looking at the rows of chocolate bars

displayed at the front of the counter, and his mouth watered. His old love of sweets had never diminished. He would have two bars, he decided; but it never occurred to him to pay for them. All his life he had been a natural-born thief, and he had stolen every chocolate bar he had ever eaten. It was habit, custom, something that came to him naturally and unconsciously.

He used his old trick of diverting the shopkeeper's attention. He pointed to a shelf low down behind the counter. 'Is that tins of corned beef you have there?'

'Yes, John West. Do you want one?'

'Make it two tins.'

She turned round and bent down to pick up the tins, and Michael slipped two bars of chocolate from the display counter into his pocket.

'Oh, listen, tell you what,' he said, 'will you hold on to them for me? I'll buy them later, on my way back. Save me lugging them around on the bike.'

'I will, of course,' she smiled agreeably. She leaned forward to get a better look at the Kawasaki parked on the road outside. 'That's a grand machine you have. I wish I had your speed.'

'Ah, sure, it gets me around.' Michael turned to leave. 'Good luck.'

'Bye. See you later.'

He wheeled the bike further down the road, so he was out of her view, then parked it near a wall and sat on it. He took out one of the stolen bars of chocolate and munched it contentedly.

Fresh air, country people, the long and winding road, a few grand in your pocket, delicious chocolate bars — what more could a dead man ask for?

He grinned his famous grin as he thought about it all — the big triumphs, the little scams; all in the game. But this latest scam of his would be his biggest triumph yet.

He laughed to himself as he imagined Noel Quigley's face.

Ah, Jesus, he'd forgotten to buy the postage stamp!

He flicked away the wrapping from the chocolate bar, reached into an inner pocket of his jacket and took out a postcard. He had bought it in the last town.

A postcard of Caravaggio's *The Taking of Christ*, in all its splendid colours. The cards were on sale everywhere and had been selling in their thousands, ever since the destruction of the original masterpiece.

All that was left to the nation now was the replica in the Jesuit Community House, and there it would stay. The priests had refused to give that up to anyone — especially after they heard how the gardaí had treated the original masterpiece, shooting it to shreds.

Father Grogan had spoken on TV, very angry, appalled, horrified — he had run out of words to describe his 'disapprobation of such a violent act against a great work of art'.

He refused to allow the press — or anyone — to enter the Jesuit House to take a photograph of the replica, the only souvenir of *The Taking of Christ* they had left.

The gardaí had apologised for the loss, but justified it as being unfortunate but nevertheless necessary: the lives of police officers had been in grave danger, and surely no painting was worth the loss of a man's life. The fact that Stevie Brady and Alec Duignan had died in the operation was something they glossed over. Two criminals, who had been menaces to society and were also reputed to have been members of the IRA.

That had been two weeks ago, and now all the media interest in the subject of the destroyed painting had died down. But everyone wanted to have either a poster or a postcard to remind them of the masterpiece and the great story of criminals that went with it.

Michael smiled. That was all to his benefit. The news of the destruction of the Caravaggio had gone all round the world, so it was no longer hot stolen property that no one wanted to buy. It was saleable again, in that secret collectors' world where any art expert could authenticate it as the original. What a coup for whoever bought it! And the price would now be millions.

He sat back, looked around at the peaceful green countryside and started dreaming, planning... To get a fake passport in a false name would be easy. He knew how and where. Then he would do what most criminals do, and go to Spain.

He would rent or buy two villas in the Costa del Sol and arrange for Christine and Lisa and the kids to join him. After that, he would plan all his future jobs in the sunshine.

Beforehand, of course, he would steal the genuine Caravaggio from the Jesuit House and conceal it inside a mirror, as before. He was the only man in the world who knew it was the original, and that was the best ace he had ever kept up his sleeve.

He sat for a long time thinking over his latest master plan, all the little details of how it could and would be done...

It was a while before he even noticed the young boy standing beside him, his eyes roving admiringly over the Kawasaki.

'Hey, little fella.'

The boy was about ten years old, and agog. 'God, that's a great bike, isn't it? How much did it cost you?'

'A lot.'

'I'm saving up to buy a motorbike when I'm sixteen.'

'How much have you saved?'

'Eight pounds and thirty-three pence.'

'Would you like to earn another pound?'

'A pound — wicked!' The boy laughed. 'D'yeh mean it?'

'Sure I do.' Michael put his hand in his pocket and took out a handful of change. 'Here's a pound, and here's another thirty-two pence. Go back to that general store there and get me a stamp, will you.'

The boy zoomed off like a firecracker, and zoomed back holding a stamp.

Michael stuck it on the Caravaggio postcard. 'Now run back and put it in the box for me.'

He watched the boy running back to the post-box and dropping it inside without even looking at it.

The lad ran back to him hopefully. 'You got any other jobs yeh want me to do?'

'No.'

Michael put his helmet on and started up the bike. He paused for a second, looking at the boy, remembering himself at that age — always hungry and eager to grab any penny he could to buy sweets.

He put his hand in his pocket and took out another pound. 'But sure,' he said, 'you only live once, so why be mean?' He flicked the coin in the air. 'Here's another pound.'

'Wicked!'

He drove off at speed, smiling to himself as he thought of the postcard. It should arrive in Dublin tomorrow or the day after.

Chapter Thirty-One

I n the refectory of the Jesuit House, Father Grogan and
his fellow priests were seated at the long table, their
heads bowed in prayer.

Life had returned to its old routine. There was no more
talk of the National Gallery or the destruction of the
Caravaggio original. Father Grogan had forbidden it.
What was the purpose in feeling resentment or anger?
They must rise from being miserable to being exalted, for
material possessions meant nothing to them. Peace and
truth and doing the good work of God were all that truly
mattered — all that they had dedicated their lives to.

Minutes later they commenced their breakfast, enjoying the warm bread-rolls and hot tea. They paid no
attention to *The Taking of Christ*; once again, they were
happily oblivious to the treasure hanging on the wall
behind them.

*

Three miles across the city, Noel Quigley was walking
cheerfully down the hall of his house to pick up the post
from the floor.

He flicked through it: a letter for his wife from her

sister in Canada, a bill from the Electricity Board, and a postcard.

He stared at the picture: Caravaggio's *The Taking of Christ*.

His heart began to pound, his pulse racing. Even before he turned it over, he knew who it was from.

It was not signed; just a few words penned in blue Biro, words from the song he had heard at the funeral.

You left without even closing the door
I didn't stand in your way...

He stared helplessly at the postcard, realising that he, Noel Quigley, had played right into Michael Lynch's hands by cancelling all surveillance, wiping all details of Lynch from the gardaí's computer screen, and officially burying him.

And that was just what Michael Lynch had wanted him to do.

The TV cameras had recorded his funeral for the people of Ireland to see, so any further major robberies or masterminded scams could not be charged to Michael Lynch — a dead man the gardaí had personally buried.

Noel slumped back against the wall and, irrationally, found himself smiling. For the first time he felt a sliver of respect for his adversary, who had outmanoeuvred him again.

He looked down at the postcard in his hand and muttered, 'God damn you, Michael Lynch, you bastard.'